THE TANGLED WEB OF TIME

THE TANGLED WEB OF TIME

BRIAN STABLEFORD

WILDSIDE PRESS

ACKNOWLEDGEMENTS

I am very grateful to Antonio Vargas for kindly letting me have a copy of his excellent paper on "Freedom under the Laws of Fate in Proclus," which he read at the Prometheus Trust Conference in June 2016, and some of his further observations on the subject. I am also grateful to Crystal Addey, whose similarly fascinating paper at same conference on "Sosipatra, Destiny and Death" also provided some inspiration for the present novel. They are not, of course, in any way responsible for the strange fictional directions in which I have run with the ideas in question. The flashback sequences in the novel are loosely based on a story entitled "Regression," published in the April 2000 issue of *Asimov's Science Fiction*.

—BS

Published by Wildside Press LLC.
www.wildsidepress.com

I

I stepped out of the school gate, as usual, and turned left, as usual, to begin the three-quarter mile, fifteen minute walk home, carrying my briefcase, as usual, and suddenly found Jimmy McKinnon standing in front of me.

The years seemed to melt away, abruptly, but not in a straightforward way. The sight of him might, and perhaps ought to, have taken me back ten years, to the moment in 2006 when I had last seen him, and had told him, in a fit of petulance, that I never wanted to see him again. But it also took me back twenty years, and thirty, to the other episodes in our personal history, abruptly linking them up and changing the temporal dots into a sequence. And as soon as it was a sequence, the ten year gap that separated me from that last time appeared as just that—a gap in a more complicated pattern—and the sight that was so very unexpected acquired a curious simultaneous sense of the inevitable, as if it were somehow fated that I was always going to bump into Jimmy at ten year intervals, approximately if not precisely.

By virtue of the same inversion of perspective, those encounters with Jimmy—which would have seemed, if the thought of him had crossed my mind a day or a week or a year before to be exotic and slightly uncomfortable lacunae in my orderly and thoroughly disciplined personal history—were suddenly highlighted in my memory. It was as if they constituted the true history of my life, while the long, stable, controlled periods in between were the real lacunae: the phases of my existence in which the gears of my presence in the world were somehow not engaged.

That was absurd, of course—but sudden shocks can affect you that way. Not that I had time to think about it at leisure, because I had a decision to make, and make *immediately*. The past, which had been remote a moment before, had caught up with me, and had overtaken me; I had to decide how I felt about that, and depending on how I felt, I had to react. Having had no warning, and no time to prepare a potential response, I had to decide where Jimmy McKinnon figured in my life, and whether he ought to figure there at all in the future.

The idea uppermost in my mind, the instant that recognition set in, was the all-too-clear memory that the last words I had spoken to him, or very nearly the last, were "Never again, Jimmy." I had meant it at the time, obviously, but I had spoken in the heat of the moment, under stress. The question was: did I still mean it? That was what I had to figure out—and instantly. Should I allow the seemingly molten years to cast me ashore on that precise moment, with all its bitterness, or should I let them carry me back to some earlier phase of our friendship—the first, especially—when I had felt quite different?

In my confusion, I honestly didn't know. I had to interrogate myself, and see how I felt. I had no idea, obviously, what might hang on that investigation and that discovery, but I felt, even at the time, that it was important, that I really ought to try to get it right.

And I found, when I looked into myself to see how I felt—perhaps somewhat to my surprise—that I was glad to see him.

I hadn't forgotten that I hadn't wanted to see him again, or why I hadn't, but somehow, that determination had melted away with the time elapsed, and the reconnection I made when I saw Jimmy standing there on the pavement wasn't with the moment that I had been horribly angry with him—and, let's admit it, frightened of him—but with three whole years of moments some eighteen to twenty years before that, when we were at university together, when we were close friends, perhaps meta-phorical blood-brothers, albeit as far from identical twins as any imaginable people of the same age could be.

We are the same age, in fact. We were born on the same day, within a couple of hours of one another, only a couple of hundred miles apart. In the context of crude astrological understanding, we should have been marked down for similar personalities and similar fates…except that what's really written in the stars is infinitely more complicated than that, if you believe…but I don't.

He didn't say anything. He just waited. He wanted to see my reaction before he decided to act. From his viewpoint, that was the right way round.

"My God, Jim," I said—because I remembered that he didn't like to be called Jimmy any more, even though I always had and always will think of him as Jimmy—"you look terrible."

He did look as if he'd been ill, but to tell the truth, he mostly looked grotesquely out of place.

"Thanks, Mark," he said, half-smiling, more in relief than amusement, because I hadn't cut him dead or told him to go to hell. "You, on the other hand, look just the same, barring a few gray hairs. Clean living, I guess. You're late, though."

He looked at his wristwatch as he said it Wearing a wristwatch isn't enough, yet, to make a person seem out of time; lots of people, especially those of our generation, still wear watches as well as carrying mobile phones, but the gesture somehow seemed to emphasize the fact that he had emerged from the past—ultimately and essentially, in fact, from the 1980s, when everybody wore a wristwatch because mobile phones were still thin on the ground, and were only used for making phone calls.

"Actually, I'm not," I said. "Although the pupils' teaching day still finishes at four, half the kids stay on for various clubs and activities, and a teacher's day now extends to contractually to five—and to tell you the truth, it's a rare day that I'm able to get away on the dot; on days when Claire works late, I tend to stay on until six...."

I stopped, suppressing the temptation to add even more layers of futile explanation, as if I somehow owed him an apology for not having been punctual at an appointment we'd never made, because I had never expected to see him again.

"It's doesn't matter," he assured me, complementing the half-smile with a nod of the head that might have been a tentative attempt at an apology on his behalf. "I'm sorry I didn't call, but...well, let's say that I wanted to surprise you. And I'm sorry I look terrible—I didn't mean to frighten you."

There were still pupils filtering through the gate in ones and twos, heading home after after-school activities, and they all looked at us curiously as they sidled past, probably not so much startled by the strange yellow-brown color of Jimmy's complexion as the outfit he was wearing. I was conforming to dress code, in a dark suit and tie with polished shoes—even though we were nearing the end of term and the end of the school year, and the July heat-wave was just getting under way, the code never relaxed—but he was clad in a shapeless khaki jacket, slightly crumpled trousers of the same color and the kind of boots that allow you to step on snakes and scorpions with impunity. He looked like a man who had just returned from a long safari—as, I supposed, he had, in a way. He even had a broad-brimmed hat—although that, admittedly, was a sensible precaution, given the way that the sun was beating down, even at five o'clock. We were only three weeks away from the solstice. I rather wished I had a hat myself, or even a mortar board.

Personally, I thought he looked like Allan Quatermain—but that merely illustrated that I was a historian, mentally living before my own time. To whom must the boys have likened him? Indiana Jones? I realized, with a slight sinking feeling, that the generations of schoolboys pass so quickly that for the pupils giving us sidelong glances, even Indiana Jones was someone retired to the remote past, known only to their parents. If any cultural icon had replaced him in their newly-expanding consciousness, I had no idea who it might be.

"You didn't frighten me, Jim," I assured him. "It's good to see you again, and you don't look terrible at all. But...."

"The after-effects of a nasty tropical bug," he hastened to assured me, quick to infer that I might be wondering—as, in fact, I was—whether the damage evident in his features might self-inflicted. "Actually, I'm looking a lot better. If you'd seen me three weeks ago…in fact, I *am* better—the doctors at St. Thomas's ran me through every test they could think of, and a few extra ones ordered by the Company, which haven't reached their standard repertoire yet. I'm fine. I nearly had a relapse when they flew me home, but I'm fine—and the only drugs I've taken, not just for the last month but for years, are the ones the doctors have forced on me."

I nodded, to signify that I would take his word for that, and that I approved. I did approve, although I suspended judgment, for the moment, as to whether I really believed him.

I had, of course, been comparing him with the old Jimmy, and my initial snap judgment that he looked "terrible" was comparative. Looked at clinically, as I tried to do now that the surprise had worn off, I supposed, he still qualified as a handsome man, albeit more ruggedly than before, and I didn't suppose for a moment that he'd lost the old charm, the mysterious charisma. Indeed, the tropical explorer look probably added to his ambience in at least some female eyes.

"I'm glad you've got over it," I told him. "What was it? Malaria? Yellow fever?"

"Been there, done that, built up the immunity," he said. "Same general family as yellow fever, I suppose, and you can obviously still see the yellow, but it bulldozed straight through twenty years of carefully-accumulated antibodies. The MSF team at Jiwaka assured me that they'd seen it before, but there are so many different bugs producing similar symptoms that they don't bother giving them distinct names. The Company takes a different view, of course; they'll want it Latinized and filed away. If it turns out not to be on file, once they've sequenced the cultures, they might even name it after me: *Jiwakanastius mckinnonensis*, or something similar. Sorry—my Latin's never been up to scratch."

"Where's Jiwaka?" I asked. My geography had never been up to scratch, and I had no idea what continent Jimmy had been on lately.

"Papua New Guinea, up in the mountains. Not quite civilization's last outpost—although, you'd probably think it was somewhere beyond that—but the last stop on the trail to remote tribal territory. Things like this are just hazards of the profession." He stroked his cheek with the middle-finger of his right hand, as if to wipe away the unhealthy coloration, which didn't even smear. "The trouble with hunting new species is that you can't just find the plants, and from the viewpoint of the invisible parasites, strangers are juicy fresh meat. What was it Nietzsche said about looking into the abyss? I forget.

"Anyhow, the miracles of modern medicine can cope, heroically, even in field-hospitals operated by Médecins Sans Frontières in the back of beyond, if the poor fellows carrying you can get you there in time. I really owe those guys, even more than the medics, and…well, the nurses. I sustained a little liver damage—hence the remnants of jaundice—and there's no other slimming aid quite like dysentery, but I'm on the mend. I could go back, but the Company lawyers won't have it. A couple of months' compulsory rest and recuperation, to clear them on their duty of care. Hence the leave; hence the return to Blighty; hence…well, here I am, at the risk of being told to go away and never darken this stretch of pavement again, in case you really meant what you said when we parted last."

"I meant it," I told him.

His face fell, insofar as a gaunt, jaundiced face whose complexion gives new meaning to the expression "weather-beaten" can fall.

"But I don't any more," I added.

And he smiled—not a half-smile, this time, but the whole thing: one of his old smiles. To the kids still strolling past, with the special kind of insolent indolence that only teenage boys possess, wondering what the hell the Head of History was doing talking to some dead-beat from an old action-adventure movie, it would just have been a broad but lop-sided smile, but to me it was a bridge across the years, a link to my own youth.

That smile, more than anything else, seemed to confirm the molten liquidity of the past, because it took me all the way back on the memory-train to what seemed, from my current standpoint in life, to have been a kind of Golden Age: not just the time when we had formed our bonds, but the time when the forging of such bonds had been possible, and natural. I had other bonds now, obviously, ones that were much tighter and infinitely more stable, and I hadn't entirely lost the capacity to form more—but not the way I had in the Golden Age of adolescence. There could never be another Jimmy.

The smile also told me that even though my astrological twin was a year over fifty, exactly as I was, and even though he looked like a man recovering from the aftermath of a spell in a Médecins San Frontières field hospital in the remotest depths of Indonesia, Jimmy McKinnon really had retained his personal magnetism: the enigmatic quality that, even though he wasn't, strictly speaking, particularly handsome or un-duly tall, differentiated him not merely from me but from the majority of male human beings.

It also reminded me of the fact that he had to have some kind of agenda, that he wasn't lurking outside the school gate in fancy dress, waiting for an old friend to start his ritual walk home, simply in order to say hello, and to beg forgiveness for the last time they'd met. Jimmy wasn't the kind of person just to appear out of the blue after ten years just to say hello. Is anyone? He wanted something, and the reason for that smile wasn't so much the fact that he was pleased to see me, and pleased that I no longer wanted never to see him again, but because he now felt sure that he was going to get whatever it was he wanted, once he got around to asking.

"If I remember correctly," he said, "There used to be a distinct dearth of pubs in the vicinity, but if things have changed, I'd be glad to buy you a drink." The sidelong glances of the belated uniformed boys had apparently begun to make him feel a trifle uncomfortable standing outside the gate, or at least a trifle conspicuous.

Things hadn't changed, though. The dearth of pubs was because most of the local land had been owned by Quakers back in the nineteenth century, and history has its inbuilt inertia, but the school would have strongly opposed any application to open licensed premises in its vicinity anyway. It wasn't the only school in the area; its effective counterpart, the girls' school that Melody attended, was only a quarter of a mile away, and their respective heads made up a formidable lobby, of which members of the borough council walked in respect, if not in fear.

"There's a coffee shop on Mount Pleasant," I said. "It's part of a chain but perfectly tolerable. You can buy me a double espresso if you like—I can always use one."

"Hard day at the chalk-face?" he asked, sarcastically.

"Haven't seen a chalk-face for some time," I told him, as we started walking toward Mount Pleasant. It was a little out of my way, but my usual route home was entirely composed of residential streets, except for a couple of minimarkets. "The job's almost all admin nowadays: paperwork, organizing and collating, and implementing incessant government initiatives. I only teach the sixth, and the whiteboards and blackboards of yore have all gone. Even PowerPoint's days are numbered. It's the devil's own job keeping up."

"Even teaching history has been computerized and visualized, then?" he observed, just to be polite and seem interested.

"Like you wouldn't believe," I said. "Mind you, being able to get access to original documents on line—the Domesday Book, the Magna Carta and records of births, marriage and deaths by the cartload—has its advantages...."

I didn't bother going on. Jimmy had never been interested in documents, whether parchment, paper or electronic. That had always been one of the contrasts between us. He was a practical man, through and through, all fieldwork, lab analysis and active experimentation. In the days when computers still churned out reams of paper print-outs, even in his line of work, and he still been based in England, required to plow through stacks of the stuff, he'd been a man at sea, a man in danger of drowning. Now…well, I really couldn't imagine what life must be like for him now, out in one or other of the last new fragments of jungle wilderness left on the Earth's surface. I had no mental apparatus with which to picture it, or even any stored-up fictional archetypes to which to compare it.

"I didn't know you were in Indonesia," I told him—although he knew that, because he had to be perfectly well aware that he hadn't bothered to inform me of the fact. "If I'd thought about you at all in these last ten years, I'd have presumed that you were still in Brazil, or somewhere else in South America, dodging piranhas and living on coca leaves." That was slightly malicious, but it bounced off. It took more to make Jimmy feel offended than a sly suggestion that you hadn't given him a thought for ten years, or that he might have been living on unrefined cocaine.

"Everybody and his cousin is up the Amazon these days," he told me, airily. "It's practically tourist territory. Mind you, parts of Indonesia aren't much better—Borneo particularly. Some of the smaller islands are biologically fascinating, but ethnomedically speaking, Papua New Guinea is the world's last almost-untouched resource. There are no more first contacts to be made, alas, and the so-called stone-age cultures discovered there in the twentieth century were never as completely isolated as the anthropologists liked to pretend, but still…there's real scope for discovery there."

"Can't wait to get back, then, once the Company suits have cleared you for action?" I suggested.

"To tell the truth," he said. "I'm not entirely sorry to be confined to the Blighty bench for three months. If I've become seriously frustrated with the suits it's because of the hoops they've been making me jump through since I got back. As I said, they really put me through the testing mill, and as soon as I was allowed out of St. Tom's, they had me out at Basingstoke for what they called a thorough debriefing. If I had a choice between lying at death's door on a camp bed in an MSF tent in the back of beyond, shitting out my insides and raving with delirium, on the one hand, and going over seven years of reports with a bunch of lab-stool nitpickers in Basingstoke on the other…well, let's just say that it wouldn't be as easy a decision as you might imagine. The doctors are bad enough, but once the Company lawyers and accountants have you in their carefully-sterilized grip, you might as well be in a straitjacket. It's over now, though, and I can get on with…my life."

He still wasn't quite ready to say what he'd almost said instead of "my life," and I was in no hurry. I certainly wasn't going to bring up his obsession before he did, even if it would make it easier for him if he could judge my reaction in advance, before he launched his gambit.

I figured that if the Great Work, the Grail Quest, was why he had ambushed me—and I had no doubt at all that it was—then he'd get to it soon enough, as soon as he felt that he'd done his duty politeness-wise. Personally, I was perfectly happy to take things one at a time, to linger upon other matters indefinitely.

Jimmy's personal philosopher's stone wasn't the only topic I wanted to avoid, though. I had already made a mental note to the effect that I ought not to mention the word "biopiracy" either, because I wasn't entirely sure how Jimmy would react to it; it hadn't been current last time I'd seen him. He'd just described his field as "ethnomedicine," which has a nice academic ring to it, but Jimmy wasn't an academic; he was a practical man. When he'd left university with his upper second in biochemistry, graduating on the same day as me, he'd gone straight into what people were already beginning to call "Big Pharma" even in the late eighties, and he'd been there ever since. Professionally, at least, he was part of what many people saw as a rather unsavory exploitation machine, and his assiduous searching for elements of the idiosyncratic pharmacopeias of preliterate that might offer new source of patentable and marketable medicines for the chronic ailments of "the West" was something that attracted a good deal of abuse in certain sectors of the chattering classes.

I wasn't sure how I felt myself about the fact that my oldest friend had devoted his career to sticking his grubby hands into places where the white man's foot had hardly trod before, in order to see what he could filch, rather than for the pure intellectual joy of accumulating exotic data. On the other hand, at the end of the day, what he was looking for among the idiosyncratic cultural uses of rare plants—at the literal risk of his life, apparently—were effective treatments for diseases, instruments for the relief of suffering. The fact that they were appropriated, patented, monopolized—at least for while—and marketed along the way was just the price of the operation, the rough that one proverbially has to take with the smooth.

At any rate, I thought it was a topic of conversation best avoided for the time being, while we still had safer ones through which to plow—and it wasn't as if Jimmy was a Company man through and through, In fact, as he's just demonstrated graphically, he loathed the Company. He didn't work for the minions of Big Pharma because he loved them, but because it facilitated his private agenda, his personal quest. His employers surely knew that—but in all probability, they didn't mind it in the least; indeed, if my understanding of the workings of the distant and alien world of Private Scientific Enterprise was correct, they almost certainly encouraged it, in accordance with a long-established policy: keep the geeks happy by giving them space to ride their hobby-horses, and they'll be all the more eager to deliver the goods for you as well.

And there were reasons, too, why Big Pharma might be very interested, albeit on the sly, in Jimmy's particular hobby-horse, even if they weren't quite the same reasons for his own interest in it. Jimmy's hobby-horse was a trifle more spirited than most, and considerably more hazardous to ride, but I felt sure that the company lawyers who were taking such an interest in his full recovery had carefully screened their employers from any and all liabilities in that direction. Paying for his legitimate medical expenses when he suffered from the occasional inevitable bout of some tropical disease as the abyssal parasites found him out was one thing, but when he risked his life in other ways....

We had turned left into Mount Pleasant; the coffee shop was practically on the corner. It was usually crowded between five and six, but it was a Monday in July and it was hot—"glorious," some would have called it, but not me—so a substantial cohort of the regulars had moved to the ice-cream parlor, or had headed for the patch of grass over the other side of the road that the local borough council, showing a rare sense of irony, had the nerve to call a "park." All the tables on the street were full, but there were empty seats inside.

Crossing the threshold evidently seemed to constitute some kind of boundary line in Jimmy's estimation of propriety, because he seemed to draw himself up to his full height, took off his hat and waved it in the direction of the corner of the room in a vague but authoritative manner. "Right," he said. "You grab that table and I'll get you that espresso. As you said, you might need it."

His tone was light and breezy, almost seductive—but I knew that however it sounded, and however he intended it, from my point of view, it contained a threat.

II

It had been just a couple of months short of thirty years before, in September 1986, that I had first met Jimmy McKinnon. It was our first day at university, and we had both acquired rooms in a three-story house shared by seven students. He and I got the two rooms on the top floor, our doors facing one another at the top of a narrow staircase. They were the same size and identically furnished, after the standard pattern of student rooms: a single bed, a desk, an armchair, a sink, a fitted wardrobe and a chest of drawers. The walls were painted cream in similarly identical fashion, but by the time we got around to introducing ourselves to one another, his had been transformed by numerous brightly-colored posters, whereas mine were still off-white and naked, and his room had already acquired a typical untidiness, with miraculous alacrity, while mine was already subject to the order and control that reflected my very different personality.

It only took us a week or so to discover that we were "astrological twins," save for a trivial matter of minutes and miles, but by that time we already knew that we were chalk and cheese. I was from the home counties, whereas Jimmy was from way up north—not actually Scotland, in spite of his name, but not so very far away—and I had been a middling pupil at an all boys' grammar school of high reputation, whereas he had been the intellectual star of his local comprehensive. My father worked for the local borough council, his worked three-month shifts on a North Sea oil rig. I was studying history, which had always been my favorite subject at school, along with English Literature; he was doing biochemistry, having specialized in sciences since turning sixteen. He was dark-haired and brown-eyed; I was fair-haired and blue eyed. We were both of middling height, with no more than an inch of difference between us, but he was sturdy and muscular, whereas I was slim and bespectacled. He was, in pseudopsychological terminology, an extrovert, and then some, whereas I was a classic introvert, and then some.

I suppose, insofar as either of us was responsible for the friendship that developed, it was him, but it wasn't something he set out to cultivate consciously. He didn't choose me, any more than I chose him. It was as if his personality was so large and expansive that it simply drew me in, automatically, because I lived opposite the stair-head. He simply absorbed me into the things he did, and allotted me a role therein. From the very beginning, I think, he employed me as a kind of counterweight, a balancing factor—not so much to slow him down, although it didn't take him long to start calling me his "brake-man"—but simply to keep him balanced and stop him flying off at a tangent. When we went out drinking together, as we often did, there was never any nonsense about buying rounds or competing; it was always understood that I would stay moderately sober, whether he did or not. In all fairness, he often did; we were students, after all, and experts at the difficult art of making a pint of anything at all last far longer than necessary or reasonable.

There were circumstances in which the difference of temperament between us proved useful, at least to him. It allowed us to become a kind of conversational double-act in which he was the comedian and I was the straight man, feeding him the cues that permitted him to indulge and develop his personal magnetism. He quickly pointed out to me an interesting sociological fact—at least, he thought it was a fact—whereby girls who were available for chatting up almost invariably went out in pairs, composed of one attractive girl and one noticeably dowdier one, who made the attractive one seem even more attractive by comparison. The practical art of seduction, he explained to me, mostly consisted of deflecting the attention, and eventually getting rid of the dowdy one, so that the "target" was left exposed. My job, as his "wing-man," was to engage, monopolize and ultimately detach the dowdy one, whose favors might eventually fall to me, much as the curée of a successful hunt might be thrown to the pack.

It worked, too, although much more satisfactorily, on the whole, from his point of view than mine. I didn't mind, or I told myself I didn't; I wasn't interested in simply scoring notches on the bed-head; I always told myself that the real aim of the game was to wait, attentively but patiently, until the right woman came along, and then settle down with her, provided that she was of the same mind. That's what I did, and never regretted doing it. Jimmy, as might be expected, married in his twenties and again in his thirties, in the red heat of passion, and got divorced after seven years both times, in the blue chill of bitter acrimony. He blamed the demands of his job both times, but I was never convinced that it would have been any different whatever he was doing—and while he was with Vanessa, at least, he was still home-based, spending his days in the same lab and going home every evening when he clocked off. Except, of course, that he didn't go home every evening when he clocked off, to settle down in front of the TV. A person like Jimmy could never have coped with that kind of dull regularity.

In matters of wine, women and song—or beer, sex and rock and roll, as he would probably have phrased it—there was never any dissent between us. We didn't necessarily drink the same kinds of alcohol or like the same kinds of music, any more than we supported the same football team, and although we did like the same kinds of women, I knew my limitations, so there was no real source of friction, no sharp-edged bones of contention. There was tension in our friendship, of course, but it was what Charles Atlas, back in the olden days, would have called "dynamic tension," the kind of tension that builds and maintains strength, not the kind of tension that causes hairline cracks that gradually spread into gaping fissures—except in one particular instance, which nearly became the rift in our particular lute.

That rift was LSD. I don't mean money—we never had much, but it was never something that caused any arguments between us—but lysergic acid ditheylamide. During the Summer Term of our second year, 1988, there was a sudden glut of the stuff circulating around the campus and going cheap. Rumor had it that someone was cooking up the stuff in the Chemistry labs, more for interest's sake than for profit, and distributing it wholesale to anyone who cared to ask. I don't know why; it was the eighties, and you'd think that a chemist interested in that sort of thing would have been brewing MDMA, which was infinitely more fashionable at the time. Jimmy swore that he didn't know who it was, but guessed that it was probably a postgrad who was able to use the labs out of hours with no questions asked. Looking back, I can't help thinking that it might even have been a member of staff already nostalgic for his own Golden Age of the sixties, but whatever the reason, the acid was there, and it was suddenly much cheaper than *es*, and in the student world, price is a major factor in decision-making.

In fact, precisely because were in the eighties, and not the sixties, people had become a trifle circumspect about LSD. A dossier of legendary acid casualties had accumulated, which didn't deter all that many people from trying it out, while it was going cheap, but did make them careful, and encourage them to take a few extra precautions: not only taking it in company, but making sure that there was someone in the company who stayed sober—the "designated driver," so to speak—who could at least try to make sure that nobody did anything too stupid.

Naturally, Jimmy wanted to try it. Equally naturally, I didn't. At first he tried to persuade me to drop some with him, just to keep him company, and even when he realized that my refusal was adamant, his first response, typically, wasn't to give up but to use all his charm and intelligence in the art of persuasion. He read up on psychedelia—not just Timothy Leary and *The Electric Kool-Aid Acid Test*, but Albert Hoffman and Richard Schultes' *Plants of the Gods* and other celebrations of shamanism—and he flatly refused to be deterred by my firm assertion that it was all "left-over hippie bullshit twenty years out of date." He simply tried to move upmarket, in literary and philosophical terms, read Aldous Huxley's *The Doors of Perception*—which was, of course, about mescaline rather than LSD, and was thirty years out of date, but the principle was the same—and adopted its title as his mantra, the lever of temptation by which he attempted to move the mountain of my obstinacy.

I don't think that Jimmy ever bothered to read William Blake's *Marriage of Heaven and Hell*, and I'm certain that he wouldn't have understood it if he had—I certainly never did—but he became exceedingly fond of quoting the passage that had inspired Huxley: "If the doors of perception were cleansed, every thing would appear to man as it is, infinite. For man has closed himself up, till he sees all things thro' narrow chinks of his cavern."

It did no good to point out to him that Huxley's particular experience had involved the objects around him taking on such an extraordinary apparent intensity that he felt almost overwhelmed by their presence, and beset by terror. Nor did it do any good to refer him to the passages in Thomas De Quincey in which he spoke of a similar overwhelming terror of the infinite as one of the effects of laudanum. He put his stress on the essay's final argument, that the quest for self-transcendence is universal, that all cultures had developed psychotropic means of trying to achieve it, and that it was just our bad luck to have been stuck with alcohol and tobacco, the worst of the bunch. LSD, he insisted, might not be perfect, but its use was a great leap forward for mankind, far more important existentially than planting footprints in the dust of the Moon.

I was having none of it. Ataraxia, I assured him—Platonic calm of mind—was what the human mind really ought to be aiming to cultivate: the ultimate victory of rational consciousness over the unruly impulses that emerge from the unconscious as passions and appetites. As good decorators, I insisted, we should be trying to fill the chinks in Blake's cavern with Polyfilla, or at the very least paper over them. The way to a happy and successful life, I insisted, was to try and make the lived-in environment of the mind as cozy and comfortable as possible, and keep it neat and tidy. Trying to open doors of perception to the infinite beyond could only be destructive, psychologically and physically, ultimately leading to madness and death, via the poisoning of the spirit and the flesh.

I can't remember how long the argument lasted—not long, I suppose; a matter of three or four intense conversations, up in our double attic, with a bottle or two of cheap wine. I thought of it at the time as a game, like many other argumentative games we had played, batting ideas back and forth like ping-pong balls, putting all the spin on them we could, although it was certainly one that I had no intention of losing.

I can't imagine that Jimmy could have taken it more seriously than that at the time; he certainly had no inkling that he was setting himself a mission for life, which would shape his career, his intellect and his personality, and bring him to the brink of madness, suicide and, if not murder, at least to within an inch of causing death by dangerous striving.

In retrospect, I suppose, it wasn't so much the LSD itself that did the damage but all the work he put into trying to get me to try it. In a way, it was my fault. If I hadn't been stubborn; if I had just shrugged my shoulders and said "Why not?" we would probably have tried it out, decided that it was over-rated, and passed on. But we didn't. For once in his life—certainly the first time, because he was certainly no lover of fiction—Jimmy was driven to read books that had little or nothing to do with science, and not just for interest's sake, but with the deliberate purpose of using their arguments as persuasive propaganda. If I hadn't resisted so hard…but that's all water under the bridge.

When he finally admitted to himself that he wasn't going to change my mind, Jimmy simply did what he usually did in negotiating the practicalities of our friendship, and changed my role within the double act. He had had time to observe that the less reckless experimenters among our fellow students would make arrangements to have a sober companion in the room while they were dropping the acid, and it was perfectly obvious that it was a role for which I was perfectly fitted. I was, after all, his brake-man; as he saw it, if I wasn't going to play the game, then I would simply have to serve as the referee. With regard to that, he simply gave me no choice, as if my refusal to try the drug itself were already a commitment to serving instead by standing and watching.

Except, as it turned out, it wasn't quite as simple as standing and watching. In practice, if not in theory, the function of the sober attendee at an acid party wasn't limited to act as a restraining influence, in case anyone took it into his or her tripped-out head to do something spectacularly stupid; it was also to report back to the trippers when they eventually woke up with a headache and a bad memory, as to what they had said and done while they were away with the fairies.

The problem with acid trips, it turned out, when our little subculture ventured into their exploration, was that the impression they often gave users of having gained some special cosmic insight, or intuited some valuable cosmic truth, rarely survived the trip. Like ordinary dreams, the substance of the trip tended to evaporate, almost entirely, once it was over and the trippers returned to their normal state of consciousness. The seemingly wonderful cosmic insights and seemingly-valuable comic truths vanished, or turned to nonsense.

Vaguely aware of the possibility that that would happen, many experimental trippers began to buttonhole their sober companions in order to communicate their insights to them while they were still fresh and alive, in order that they could be preserved and reported back to them later, when their own unreliable memories had carelessly let go of them. Sometimes, they used tape recorders, but they generally needed their sober companions to take charge of those, not just to make sure that they were switched on but also to assist in the interpretation of voice-recordings that often seemed, in retrospect, to be mere gibberish.

That aspect of the role he wanted me to play seemed particularly important to Jimmy, not simply because it would involve me more fully, but also because it would allow me to provide him with cues, just as I did in our conversational double-act. I would become not merely the recorder of his insights, but their prompter, the person who set up his punch-lines, laid the foundations for his eloquence.

"I really need you to do this Mark," Jimmy pointed out to me, even before we'd started. "I'm not just doing this in search of a quick thrill. I'm a scientist; if I'm going to do acid, then I'm going o do it seriously, in a spirit of genuine exploration—but I can't do it alone. I need a wing-man and a brake-man. I need a partner. I need someone who can guide me from outside, to help me get to where I need to go *inside*. Only you can do that; at least, you're the only one I can trust."

I was still resistant, at first. That was partly because I didn't think I was big enough and strong enough actually to stop Jimmy if he decided to believe that he could fly and took a header out of his bedroom window, but also because I could foresee trouble developing when I reported back to him what he said, even with the report of a tape recorder. If it turned out to be nonsense, as I was perfectly certain that it would, I suspected that I might get the blame, for not having guided him efficiently and effectively enough.

"Don't worry about me trying to fly," he retorted, when I raised those objections, in typical Jimmy fashion, "We'll make sure the window's locked, and we'll use my Dictaphone to record what I say, so that we can see exactly where things have gone wrong, if they do go wrong, and we can plan a strategy for the next time that will enable you to ask the right questions and provide the right prompts. Practice will make perfect."

"I don't know, Jimmy," I told him. "Once is an experiment, but 'practice makes perfect' sounds more like a career, or an addiction. This stuff is poison. Wanting to try it is understandable, but surely once will be enough."

"You're not a scientist, Mark. In fact, once is never enough. Experiments have to be replicated and repeated; that's the very essence of the method. You try things out so that you can test and improve the experimental design and the technique, and to train the operator. Obviously, there are difficulties in being both experimenter and subject, but they can be overcome, with the right auxiliary. That's you, Mark. We're a team."

Eventually, I let him convince me—because he was, of course, correct. We were a team. He did need me. And, to tell the truth, the role did have its attractions, for a historian. What a historian does is observe, from the outside—but he needs something to observe; he needs someone actually to do the things that his vocation consists of watching.

"Okay," I said, "I'm in. I'll see how it goes."

Jimmy couldn't just win the battle, of course. He had to hammer it in.

"You won't regret it, Mark, believe me. You'll be able to talk sense to me, the way you always do, and you'll enjoy that. You'll be able to keep me focused, to keep reminding me of what I'm doing and why. If the doors of perception really are there, you'll be able to help me find them focus on them and pry them open—and you'll get a real buzz out of playing your part, the way you always to. I'm doing you a big favor, Mark, taking you aboard as my wing-man in the infinite, my hyperspatial guide. But you're doing me one as well—and who else could do it as well? Who else could I possibly trust?"

That argument worked, not because of the unsubtle flattery, but because of the temptation. I really thought, when he put it like that, that I might be able to help him, that I might be able to direct his hallucination in such a way that it wouldn't be damaging and might actually be productive. Maybe, I thought, I could even supply him with some metaphorical Polyfilla and persuade him to fill in some of the cracks in his internal landscape that might some day get him into trouble.

I am not normally what one would call an optimistic person, but I was young at the time, and still a trifle foolish. Who isn't, in their Golden Age?

Perhaps it might even have worked, if Jimmy had struck to minimal doses at moderate intervals, and had approached the business of psychedelic exploration like the methodical scientist he was pretending to be, or even as a tourist with a modicum of polite decorum—but that wasn't Jimmy's way. Having tried a small dose once, with a fairly minimal effect, his immediate reaction was to that he needed to take a bigger dose, and urgently. While more tentative adolescent acid-droppers were content quietly to marvel at subtly weird distortions of perception, and to giggle gently as they were carried along by mildly bizarre trains of thought, Jimmy the alleged scientific investigator wasn't. He actually wanted to see pink elephants, if possible, and to rant and rave like a man possessed.

He didn't get addicted to LSD in any physiological sense, or even any strict psychological sense, but it certainly became more for him than a temporary fad. Maybe if the quest to overcome my reluctance hadn't led him to do all that dangerous reading…but as I said, water under the bridge.

Luckily, he didn't have much money, and, cheap as the stuff was, there was a limit to how much he could afford, even before the supply suddenly dried up. Nobody knew why; if the person doing it had been caught, the news certainly didn't leak out—but that would he perfectly understandable, if the university authorities rather than the police had done the catching, given jealous authority's instinctive love of the cover-up. Anyway, the supply was cut off as abruptly as it had come on stream, and in the meantime, even though he wasn't technically a canny Scots-man, Jimmy had the appropriate cultural proclivities, and he allowed his pocket to regulate all his adventures. In the final count, I sat with him, accompanied by his trusty Dictaphone, on at least ten occasions, maybe twelve, spread over the course of a month.

After relatively moderate beginnings, he quickly became convinced that he had not only located the doors of perception but could open them wide to reveal vistas of limitless possibility, which he became fond of calling by such pompous titles as "the wilderness of if" and "the tangled web of time"—but he also became convinced that it wouldn't be as easy as it had initially seemed, and that merely increasing the dosage wasn't going to get him over the hurdle.

Like any bad workman, he started blaming his tools—but not, ini-tially, the LSD. His first reaction, in fact, as I'd feared and anticipated, was to blame me.

"You're not doing your job, Mark," he told me, after the third or fourth failure, when he couldn't remember what had happened to him while he was away with the fairies and couldn't deduce anything coher-ent from the tape of his ramblings. "You're not providing the right cues, or asking the right questions. When I begin to go astray, you need to pin me down. You need to help me focus, to describe what I'm seeing and clarify what I'm feeling. I can't do it without you, because the experi-ence is simply too overwhelming, and I get carried away. I need a tether to anchor me to the earth, to keep a line of clear communication open."

"I try, Jimmy, I really do," I told him, "but it's like trying to grab smoke. It just isn't possible to keep you on the track. You can hear me trying, and failing. You can't tell me that I'm not making the effort"

"Of course you are," he said, softening, as he usually did. "But you obviously need more practice."

I had already decided, by that time, that I needed more practice like I needed a hole in the head, and that if he got much more, he'd probably end up with one, but if it had been difficult for me to start, it was also difficult for me to stop. I'd made a commitment—as Jimmy kept reminding me—and I was part of the team. I couldn't back out without letting him down.

The trouble was, I thought, that if I stayed in, I'd be letting him down just as badly, and perhaps with worse consequences. I was seriously worried that he was going to damage himself irreparably.

I pleaded with him to stop, but his initially reaction to my pleading was simply to laugh and to tell me that I didn't understand, and never would unless and until I tried it myself. He insisted that he'd demonstrated that there was no danger in taking it, and that there was now nothing stopping me but cowardice—and he was just as stubborn as I was in resisting my counter-argument that, far from demonstrating the harmlessness of the drug, all that he had really demonstrated was the utter pointlessness of continuing with a failed experiment that might yet become catastrophic.

I don't have the tapes now, of course, so there's no way to check, but if my memory serves me right he saw and conversed with some kind of divinity on three occasions, and that he was made party to some essential Cosmic Truth on at least half a dozen. Unfortunately, he could never reconstruct those truths afterwards; nor, in spite of my very best efforts could he contrive to acquaint me with the substance of any of them while he was in possession of them, in such a way that I could understand them. His attempted explanations were utterly incoherent, and when he eventually came crashing back to earth and avidly consulted the Dictaphone record, he couldn't understand them either.

Even before the supply ran dry, I had started praying that Jimmy would have a bad trip—not bad enough to screw him up seriously, obviously, but bad enough to scare him, sufficiently intimidating to put him off. And that, in a sense, is what happened. He did have a bad trip, not bad enough to screw him up seriously, but bad enough to scare him in a fashion that made him exceedingly reluctant to risk a repetition, and deterred him from further experimentation. Perhaps, if the supply hadn't dwindled, he might have been tempted back, and perhaps, if the final exams hadn't begun to loom up on his personal horizon in our final year, he might even have been willing to pay full price to renew the experimental run without my aid, but as things were, the combination of circumstances caused him to shelve the whole endeavor.

The incident that served as an initial punctuation-mark in that first phase of his obsession was sufficiently serious even to take the wind out of Jimmy's fully-deployed sails. Under the influence of an acid-induced delusion, he slashed my face with the scalpel from his dissecting kit and very nearly put my eye out.

I ought to make it clear right away that Jimmy didn't actually *attack* me with the scalpel. Jimmy was fundamentally a good person—and that was why the experience scared him enough to act as a deterrent. If he'd only cut himself, he would probably have shrugged it off, even if he was only a centimeter way from inflicting serious injury, but the idea that he had endangered the life, or the eyesight, of his best friend was something else. That was something that he wasn't prepared to shrug off, and wasn't prepared to risk happening again.

What Jimmy wanted to do with the scalpel when he fished it out from whichever heap of clutter in his ever-untidy room he'd carelessly left it, without my noticing—at least so far as I could gather—was to open up a channel into his head where his hypothetical third eye ought to be, so that the innate spirituality of the cosmos-at-large could flow more easily into his closeted cerebrum. Maybe he'd been reading Lobsang Rampa or some other out-of-date bullshit—how do I know?—but whatever it was, he'd somehow got hold of the idea that do-it-yourself brain surgery was the way to go, not so much to open the doors of perception but to take them off their hinges.

Perhaps I should have let him try, confident that as soon as the scalpel drew blood, the pain would make him stop, before he could actually make an incision in his cranium. But how could I be sure? In any case, the whole point of my baby-sitting him was to ensure that he didn't do anything stupid, and trying to stab himself in the middle of his forehead surely qualified as utterly stupid, by anyone's definition. Hence, it was my responsibility to stop him, if humanly possible.

There had been previous occasions when I'd been almost convinced that Jimmy was just bullshitting in the descriptions he gave of what he was allegedly seeing and feeling, making up his commentary on his hallucinations and distorted perceptions as a kind of performance, intended to make fun of the callow introvert who lived in his outgoing shadow, quietly orbiting his solar center. At first, I certainly thought that the business with the scalpel was bullshit, deliberately playing on my deepest anxieties, teasing me with calculated anxiety—but even if it started out that way, Jimmy soon fell victim to the fervor of his own patter.

I had to try to take the scalpel off him, or at least make him drop it. I literally had no choice.

And that's what I tried to do, not just because it was the responsibility I'd formally accepted, or even just because he was my best—my only—friend, but because it simply had to be done, and I was there, and that meant that I had to be the one to do it. I had no choice.

While I wrestled with him, there was no doubt in my mind that if I couldn't exert all the strength and skill that my admittedly punier arms possessed, and succeed in defeating his intention, then he would certainly do himself serious injury. In the end, though, it was me who got cut, from just beneath my right eye to the edge of my chin.

He didn't mean to do it; he was just resisting me, and resisting common sense, blindly. There was no aggression or malevolence involved. It was simply an accident.

By the time Jimmy was calm enough for me to leave him be, and I'd thrown the bloody scalpel out of his room and into mine, where it left a stain in the carpet that never did come out, I was in a bad way. I turned a white bath-towel red. I fainted in the ambulance on the way to the hospital, and eventually woke up on a drip, with seventeen stitches in my face.

That would have been bad enough, but it turned out that Jimmy's scalpel—which he had, of course, been using to cut up frogs and mice in practical classes—wasn't sterile. The wound became infected and I spent the best part of a fortnight looking like the Phantom of the Opera unmasked. The hospital nearly had to readmit me so that I could be put back on a drip, this time charged with antibiotics, but it began to clear up just in time.

Jimmy was extremely sorry, of course. He was so extremely sorry that I had no alternative but to forgive him. It's surprising how easy forgiveness comes when you're twenty years old and in your Golden Age. He swore that he would never drop acid again. He swore it on his mother's grave—but that was only figurative, given that his mother was still alive and kicking then. He meant it, though, when he actually said it, and even when he ceased to mean it, I think he stuck to the letter of it if not the spirit. To the best of my knowledge, Jimmy never did drop acid again. He just spent the rest of his life looking for something better—not safer, but better at giving access to the doors of perception, the wilderness of if and the tangled web of time.

The incident didn't spoil our friendship. There was no fall-out, no enquiry of any kind. I told everyone that I'd cut myself accidentally with a scalpel, and no one challenged the assertion, or even bothered to enquire as to what a second-year history student had been doing with a scalpel that had almost resulted in him putting his eye out. People routinely expect students to do stupid things, it seems.

I assume that Jimmy was grateful for my silence as to the circumstances of the accident, but he never actually said so, even while he was assuring me of the extent of his sorrow at having caused it. Once I had got my face back, save for a scar that Jimmy assured me only made me look "interestingly mysterious," we simply went back to doing the things we'd been doing together before the LSD fad, and didn't talk about the doors of perception again, in the context of recreational hallucinogens. But Jimmy never let go of the basic idea: the notion that human consciousness is surrounded by walls, whether defensive or imprisoning, and that the greater part of reality is located outside those walls, forbidden to the meager reportage of the five senses.

"History," he said to me once, "is an essentially narrow-minded discipline, focusing entirely on the manifest effects of human consciousness, unable to look or think beyond them. It sees time as a simple linear series of events, progressing doggedly from an unknown and presumably unimaginable beginning toward an unknown and equally unimaginable end, one tedious step at a time. But biochemistry deals entirely with a world of molecular entities and interactions beyond the reach of direct sensory perception, which we can only perceive through the intermediary of gross effects and subtle instrumentation. Those interactions are ultimately based on the strange and paradoxical intercourse of subatomic particles, ruled by quantum mechanics, by a mathematics in which the directionality of time is just an artifact of consciousness.

"History is not only essentially earthbound but essentially surface-bound; it doesn't look into things deeply, and it doesn't look outwards, into the universe beyond the earth. Biochemistry looks into things to the utmost calculable depths, and extrapolates its findings to speculate as to whether life exists elsewhere in the universe, and how different it might be from life on earth, within the parentheses of physicochemical theory. No wonder you and I have such different views of the world, and how one ought to live in it. No wonder you're a contented, institutionalized prisoner of consciousness, while I'm…"

But he didn't know what he was. A psychonaut? Perhaps. A traveler in the wilderness of if, boldly trying to find a way through the tangled web of time? Possibly. A restless soul? Definitely. A man incapable of finding happiness, or any kind of contentment? Maybe. But I didn't throw that last judgment in his face. I didn't want to be unkind. I didn't even try more gentle means of persuasion. To tell the truth, I wouldn't have wanted him to be like me even if I could have persuaded him to try it. I liked him for being different. I only ever argued that my *modus vivendi* was right for me, that it was the only way that I could achieve my particular aims.

"I believe you," he said, once, not long before we graduated, "when you say that it's possible for you to find happiness, or at least to manage your life in such a way as to minimize unhappiness, and I certainly don't begrudge you that. But I can't bring myself to envy you, let alone to try to do likewise. I can't. I couldn't."

"I know," I told him.

"Burt we'll always be friends," he said, with conviction. "In a matter of weeks, we'll be going our separate ways. You'll get a job in your field, I'll get one in mine. They'll send us in very different directions, perhaps to different continents. Perhaps we'll lose touch. But we'll always have these three years in our memory, as a crucial turning-point in our lives. We'll always have this bond."

"We won't lose touch," I told him. "I'll make sure we stay in communication, even if we're on different continents."

That was a promise I failed dismally to keep. To the limited extent that we did keep in touch, it was Jimmy who did the keeping. He was the one who sent postcards, who made occasional phone calls, and who turned up, admittedly at long intervals, to remind me that we were still friends, and to tell me that I was still his wing-man, still his brake-man, because he'd never found anyone else he could trust with that responsibility. He never actually said in so many words that he'd never find anyone else who would try so determinedly to stop him digging a hole in his head, at the risk of having his eye put out and contracting a dangerous infection, but that was what he meant. In all probability, he could easily have got someone else to do that for him, and someone big enough and strong enough to dispossess him of the scalpel without getting hurt in the process, but the point was not whether he could find someone capable of doing that, but whether he could find someone he felt that he could trust to do it.

And what was why, when he felt the need, he came back to me.

I suspect that Jimmy got through his last-minute revision for his finals on benzedrine and came down afterwards on pot—but he never asked me to keep him company when he recruited artificial aids of those sorts. I didn't take anything, but I didn't leave things to the last minute either, and the ultimate result was the same in either case, as befit astrological near-twins. Throughout our final year, our relationship cruised along in the fashion I'd come to think of as normal, with a frugal but nevertheless adequate ration of wine, women and song—adequate, at least, from my point of view. Occasionally, however, I saw him wince shamefacedly when his gaze was caught by the scar I bore. It took a long time to fade, and can still be discerned if you look closely.

The goodbyes we said after the graduation ceremony were inhibited by the presence of our two sets of parents. I certainly hadn't told mine that Jimmy was responsible for the injury to my face but they seemed to have caught on somehow that he had been involved—or perhaps they simply didn't like him. At any rate, there was a distinct frostiness about their handshakes. When we parted and went our separate ways I felt that a phase of my life had come to an end, and that a different one was about to begin—that the Golden Age had given way to the Age of Iron—and I was right. If you stick to feelings of that obvious sort, you rarely go wrong. Mostly, I did. Mostly, I still do.

Over time, the scar faded, although, as I say, it never entirely disappeared.

With luck, I suppose, that might have been the end of the matter, but everyone knows the old saying about those who fail to learn from history being condemned to repeat it, first as tragedy and then as farce—and perhaps, on occasion, it works the other way around.

III

I sat down in a corner of the coffee shop, and I collected myself. Jimmy ordered the coffees, paid for them and ferried them over to the table with due care and attention. His hands didn't seem unduly unsteady as he made the brief trip. Naturally, he had bought himself a cappuccino. Contrasts, always contrasts.

"How's Claire?" he asked, politely, when he sat down. Apparently, he had decided that a little more polite chitchat was in order before he got down to the reason why we were there.

"Thriving," I assured him.

"Still working for the National Health Service?"

"Yes—but she's moved departments a lot more than I have, and she's been promoted further and faster. She's way up in the stratosphere of the hospital trust now—she has even more paperwork than me to read and produce, and far more committee meetings to attend. I couldn't cope with it myself—and you can imagine the pressure, with the constant budget cuts, the avalanche of performance targets and the blizzard of lawsuits."

"Actually, no," he said. "Having been away for such a long time...."

"Well," I said, "it's bad. People at her level are dropping like flies from the stress, but not Claire. She's organized, and she cuts through all of it, straight as a die. She's magnificent."

"Still in love, then?" he commented—not maliciously at all, merely checking.

"Absolutely." I'd been past thirty before I actually tied the knot, although we'd been seeing one another for quite a while beforehand. I always said previously that I was waiting until I found the right woman, and even though that had been partly a defensive move, an excuse for lack of headway on life's snakes-and-ladders board, things really had worked out that way. Eventually, I had found the right woman, perhaps, in hindsight, more by luck than judgment, but nevertheless....

"And Melody?"

I was oddly grateful that Jimmy had remembered my daughter's name, only having met her very briefly, when she was eight.

"Off to university in September, assuming that the exam results come up to expectation," I told him. "It'll be a bit of a wrench, I expect—

the house will seem empty without her—but time marches on, and they grow up, and things have to take their course."

"Is she pretty?" Jimmy asked. Typical Jimmy. Not "What is she going to study at university?" but "Is she pretty?"

"About average, I guess," I said, defensively. I didn't want Jimmy to get the idea that Melody was pretty, not because…well, actually, yes, precisely *because*. Not that there was anything to worry about. Jimmy was my friend. He hadn't made any attempt to seduce my wife ten years before, and he wouldn't have done so even if I hadn't cut the encounter short by telling him that I never wanted to see him again. He certainly wasn't going to seduce my daughter. Not deliberately, anyhow.

Rapidly, I said: "How about you? Any more marriages, children, divorces?"

The last time I'd seen him, Jimmy was married for the second time, to Julie, but it was already approaching the rocks, with divorce inevitable. He had no children from that marriage or from his earlier one to Vanessa. I half-expected him to have completed the holy hat-trick during an interval of a decade, but apparently not.

"No," he said. "I decided after Julie that the job really wasn't compatible with marriage, children and the like—and two divorces is enough for any sane man."

Yes, I thought, *but*….

Aloud, I said, with contrived and supposedly humorous irony: "So you're a celibate monk of science nowadays, fully dedicated to your vocation?"

He looked slightly uncomfortable, which wasn't like him—not as I remembered him. "It doesn't work like that," he said.

"You do surprise me," I said, contriving even more irony.

"No," he said, "you don't understand what I mean. I'm not talking about my own inclinations—there's a whole culture of people working far from home, in the back of beyond: aid workers, medics, anthropologists, entrepreneurs of various sorts, and the society is as cosmopolitan as can be imagined. Obviously, we're not all alike, by any means, but the same logic of the situation applies to us all; it's not a way of life compatible with marriage, children and family, so it has its own norms of…." He couldn't find the right term.

"Sexual congress?" I suggested.

It obviously wasn't the one he would have chosen, but he shrugged his shoulders, accepting it. He was quick to add, though: "I'm with someone at the moment, though. She took her accumulated leave so that we could fly back from Indonesia together."

"Don't tell me," I said, still trying to maintain the bantering tone. "She was a nurse at the field-hospital where you were treated, and she couldn't help falling in love with you in spite of the dysentery."

For just a split second, it looked as if he might take offense, but he smiled again. "That's what I like about you, Mark," he said. "So intuitive—and you have such an elegant way of putting things. I always said you ought to be a poet rather than a historian." His tone was mild, and might almost have passed for serious.

"You mean she really is an MSF nurse and you really did meet her when you fell ill?" I said.

"Yes and no. She's more of an administrator and interpreter than a nurse, although everyone mucks in with everything out there; there aren't any pen-pushers...or keyboard-tappers, as I guess it is nowadays. And I've known her for years, as well as anyone can know anyone in our world—but you're right about my illness shifting our relationship into a higher gear. There's nothing like a sojourn at death's door, or a sojourn at the bedside of someone at death's door, to sharpen one's sense of priorities. Her name's Christiane."

"Not English, then?"

"No—but we're still in the EU, aren't we? For the time being, at least? I missed the referendum, apparently...but for the moment, she has a perfect right to be here."

"I wasn't disputing it," I assured him. "So, you suddenly decided, thanks to the bout of yellowish fever, that it was time for years of Platonic acquaintance to give way to a couple of months of bottled-up wild passion?"

"No," he said, patiently. "As I said, the culture doesn't work like that. We'd been sleeping together, on occasion, for years, and it wasn't that kind of passion that suddenly seemed urgent to us."

I almost said "What other kind is there?" but that would have been silly. I realized, a trifle belatedly, that although we were still beating around the bush, we'd got a lot closer to its center. Absurdly, I also felt a reflexive pang of jealousy.

"You mean Christiane's your new wing-man?" I said "Your current collaborator in the great Quest?"

"Yes and no," he said, again. "I mean, yes, we're collaborating—but this time, I'm the wing-man."

I actually felt a chill that was tinged with both horror and disgust. "You mean you've stopped poisoning yourself in order to start poisoning someone else—your girl-friend?" I said.

"It's not like that, Mark," he said, patiently. "At least, it is...but not in the way you make it sound. You're not seeing things in context. She's not a victim of my mad ambition and evil scheming. It's a genuine collaboration, undertaken in a rigorous scientific spirit."

"I have heard that before," I reminded him.

"And it's always been true—just as it's always been true, as I've assured you before—that as experimenters and subjects, we get better with practice. You'll see, anyway. Don't rush to judgment."

And there it was: *You'll see.* But why did he need me to see, if I'd been replaced, if he was the sober companion now, the recorder and the prompter?

I decided that I had a little more bush-beating to do myself before asking the crucial questions.

"Where are you staying?" I asked, in a neutral tone.

"In the town center, at the Premier Inn. We've been in London and Basingstoke for the last two weeks, taking care of medical fall-out and accumulated business, but everything's tidied up for the present. As soon as our time was completely our own, I wanted to look you up, in spite of…the way we left things."

"I'm glad you did," I told him, not insincerely, in spite of his recent semi-revelations.

"We couldn't leave things like that, could we?" he said, laboring the point slightly. "After all, we go back a long way, don't we?"

"Thirty years," I said. "Not exactly to the day, but…."

"I can count," he assured me. "The point is, we we're old friends, and even though life has sent us in very different directions, that old friendship still counts for something, doesn't it?"

"Yes it does," I agreed—and wondered, for the first time, whether it might have meant as much to him, and whether it might still mean as much, with the aid of hindsight, as it had meant to me, and still did, albeit with the helpful support of molten time.

"Good," he said. "It might sound stupid, I know, but I've been away from England for such a long time that I really don't know anyone here at all. I wasn't even sure that I could still claim to know you…no, that's a lie. I *was* sure of that. In spite of what you said last time, I was certain that if I turned up outside your school gate again, and waited for you, just like the last time, that you'd come out and turn left, just as you did the last time, and that you'd recognize me right away, even though I look such a wreck…and I was even sure that you'd have forgiven me, because when you'd calmed down and had time to think about it, you'd have realized that…well, that it wasn't really…."

He was about to say "me" but I cut him off. "Your fault?" I finished for him—but then I decided to be kind. "No, Jim, it wasn't entirely your fault, and was it was even more than a little bit mine. But the truth is, that it really doesn't matter whose fault it was, or whether there was a fault at all. We were friends. We still are. Even faults don't change that."

He seemed genuinely relieved—as well he might be. He could, in theory, have looked me up just, as they say "for old time's sake," given that he had a new collaborator now and didn't need me any more, but Jimmy's old time's sake always had a hidden agenda, because Jimmy always had a hidden agenda. I'm not the only person in the world who never changes; I just make my lack of change more manifest than most. Jimmy, on the other hand, had always worn all manner of mercurial disguises, as well those of world traveler, scientific soldier of fortune and serial seducer of women, whether he happened to be working in a social context intrinsically antipathetic to long-term relationships or not. Fundamentally, though, he hadn't changed.

"Thanks, Mark," he said, and left it at that. He had a smudge of cappuccino foam on his upper lip. That was one of the reasons I always ordered espresso.

I took out my phone. "I have to call Claire and explain why I'm late," I explained. "It's actually quite unusual for us both to get away from work at five, and it practically qualifies as a date when we've both scheduled the intention."

He didn't make any comment. He probably understood perfectly.

"Hi," I said, when Claire answered. "Sorry, but I'll be a bit late, I'm afraid. Best laid plans of mice and men, and all that. Ran into an old friend, and we're having a coffee on Mount Pleasant."

"Jim McKinnon?" she said, instantly.

For some reason, I felt a slight thrill of anxiety. I knew she wasn't psychic, and would never have made any such claim. She had met Jimmy exactly twice, ten years before, and I'd hardly mentioned him since, so there was a sense in which it might have been reckoned an odd conclusion for her to jump to—but she did know me very well, after nearly twenty years of marriage, and she knew, probably without having to think about it too much, or even at all, that if I used the term "old friend," there really weren't many people to whom I could be referring… and perhaps, when I came to think about it, only one. So, on due analysis, it wasn't really surprising at all that she should be able to guess who I meant even after a decade-long gap.

"That's right," I said. "He's just back from Papua New Guinea, on medical leave. Contracted something nasty up the jungle, but on the road to recovery now."

"Well, what on earth are you doing hanging around in coffee-shops on Mount Pleasant, you idiot? Bring him home, and we'll have dinner together."

I hesitated. "He's…with someone. Not actually here at this moment in time but…not in town on his own."

"Even better. Bring her too. I'll nip down to the supermarket and lay in supplies."

I looked at Jimmy, a trifle uneasily. "Claire's inviting you and Christiane to dinner," I reported.

"Great," he said. "It'll only take twenty minutes to walk into town and pick her up; then we can take a taxi to your place. Christiane isn't the type to drag things out, so we can be there in not much more than half an hour."

"Right," I said, and relayed the information to Claire, only pausing very briefly to wonder why it hadn't even occurred to me to invite him to dinner myself.

She asked about special dietary requirements, as a conscientious hostess would, and was assured that people who had spent the bulk of the last seven years working in the remoter parts of Papua New Guinea soon got used to eating whatever was available, and were generally glad to get it.

"Ask him to make it an hour," Claire said. "That way I can do the shopping and start the preparations...and you can dawdle in the coffee-shop for a while, catching up."

I relayed that information too. Jimmy nodded and took out his own phone, called his MSF matron and brought her up to date with the plan. She didn't raise any objection. Why would she?

"How old is Christiane?" I asked, curiously, as he put his phone away.

He laughed. "She's probably not what you imagine," he said. "I haven't asked, being a gentleman of sorts, but she's certainly in her late thirties, if she hasn't passed forty. She crowned Saint Catherine a long time ago."

"She's never been married, then?"

"No. As I said...."

"The lifestyle isn't conducive."

"Exactly—and she's got more common sense than me. She didn't have to learn the hard way. She got the vocation and stuck to it.

"But not exactly a nun?" I suggested.

His mouth twitched into a slight but fleeting smirk. "Not exactly, no," she said. "It's the twenty-first century, after all. We have the technology to avoid the possible complications."

"And appropriate cultural norms, it seems," I observed. "It's good of her to take her stored-up leave just to keep you company? Are you sure she hasn't fallen head-over-heels in love with you? You did have that effect on women once."

The effect wears off when you pass fifty," he said, with a contrived sigh, "And Christiane's far too sensible for that kind of romantic nonsense."

I didn't believe that for a second—on the other hand, he had assured me that theirs was a scientific collaboration, even if they had been screwing, on and off, for years. Perhaps Christiane really was capable of being as dispassionate about their relationship as Jimmy was pretending to be. But I still didn't believe it.

"Will you be going back together then when your leave ends," I asked, "and sticking it out until the call of duty eventually separates you, when MSF sends her off to the heart of Africa and Big Pharma sends you…well, God knows where?"

"We haven't made any plans," he said, in a falsely casual tone. "Out there, you tend to live in the present and take each day as it comes, because there's always so much to do just to get through to tomorrow. Mostly, you just let the leave you're due build up, and never even think about taking it, unless something stops you in your tracks like whatever parasite got into my system. It's a hard habit to lose, so, as I say, we have no definite plans, except…."

He stopped.

There was the *hic* again. There was the hidden agenda. There was the communion that he and his MSF mistress had, apart from mere sexual congress, whatever it was that Jimmy had found that might somehow qualify as a key to the doors of perception. I assumed that it wasn't the ayahuasca derivatives he'd started shooting up the last time he'd thought his job had led him to the Holy Grail, given that he was still alive, capable of surviving nasty tropical diseases and seemingly *compos mentis*. If he was shooting up anything now, apart from prescribed medications for the after-effects of his topical disease, it couldn't seem to be anything too freaky. But what was he feeding Christiane?

He wiped his upper lip with a paper napkin.

"That's the trouble with cappuccino," I observed.

"I'd forgotten," he said. He'd obviously been away from civilization for a long time.

"So, how's the work going?" I asked him. "Have you discovered the panacea yet?"

"If I had," he assured me, "I'd be sure to keep quiet about it. There's no profit in cures. You know as well as I do that what my employers want is medicines that keep people alive and completely dependent, so that they have to keep on taking them day after day and year after year, plus extra medicines to treat their side effects, and extra ones to treat the side effects of those. I'm not under any illusions about the shadier aspects of my work, so there's no need to lecture me about it from the imagined moral high ground of someone who only has to pick through the ruins of the dead past and never think about the future at all."

"Bit sharp, Jim," I said, mildly. "It really was just an innocent query."

He pulled himself together. "Yes," he said. "Sorry. Picked up bad habits hanging around with MSF and UN do-gooders. People at Christiane's level understand perfectly, of course, but some of the firebrands barge in with the best of intentions and no common sense. Well, Big Pharma isn't exactly on everybody's Christmas card list, and…have you ever heard the term biopiracy?"

"I've heard it," I said diplomatically refraining from mentioning that it had come to mind almost as soon as I'd clapped eyes on him.

"Well, it's a stupid term," he said, "but it's been a stigma I've had to wear for years now, and I guess I've become a trifle touchy about it. I'm on the side of the angels; I always have been."

I wasn't so sure, but I certainly wasn't about to deny it to his face. "Of course," I said. As a conscientious historian of course—even a mere schoolteacher imprisoned the national curriculum, with no time even for riding hobby-horses—I was strictly neutral, on nobody's side but that of the truth. Perhaps I was behind the times, even in that, given that I knew full well that what passes for history is so polluted with misinformation and disinformation that it's little more than the fantasy we choose to believe, but I was till committed to the idea that, even if the truth is forever and tantalizingly out of reach, it's the only target worth aiming for.

Jimmy would have agreed wholeheartedly with that of course; the contrast between us, immense as it was, was merely a matter how to reach the target. I had always thought of my way as the straight and narrow, and his as a bizarrely convoluted curve, but he had always disagreed, because he had spent his life looking for the paradoxical short cut that is even more direct than the straight line, because he didn't live in Euclidean mental space, but somewhere far more complicated, with far more dimensions that than human mind can really accommodate.

"How long are you planning to be in town?" I asked him.

"Haven't made any plans," he repeated. "Not long. The Company owns properties all over the place that they use to accommodate visiting scientists and other consultants on a short-term basis. HR at Basingstoke are trying to find something suitable for us to use as a base for a month or so—they keep promising news 'maybe tomorrow,' so, maybe tomorrow—but maybe not. As to whether we'll stay in one place, or play tourist alongside our serious business, I don't know. Christiane might have places she wants to see."

"Not people? In…wherever it is she comes from?"

"No, no people. She was born in Denmark, but her parents were French and Greek, both peripatetics in the EU bureaucracy, so she was schooled in various different places, even before they split up. She never really had a home, and never…well, she never formed any kind of bond like the one you and I contrived to form at uni. She envies me that, I think. She's interested to meet you."

"You've told me about her, then?"

"Obviously. You presumably talk about me to Claire, since she guessed immediately who you were with."

He was wrong about that. I didn't talk abut him. I hadn't even thought about him, for years on end…until the time had suddenly melted away. But I let him think that I had.

That must have encouraged him, or perhaps he thought that he ought to take advantage of the few minutes we still had while we were, as Claire put it "dawdling" to plant a marker, to stake a claim to the topic that was the real reason for his visit. Either way, right out of the blue, he said: "Have you ever heard of Sosipatra of Ephesus?"

I hadn't. No historian, however conscientious, has heard of everyone who ever lived. But it was the twenty-first century and the coffee-shop had free wi-fi. Without saying anything, I took my tablet out of my brief-case, and within half a minute my practiced fingers had summoned up the relevant wikipedia entry. I would probably have got there even if I'd misspelled the name, but I hadn't.

"The fourth-century neoplatonist philosopher and mystic featured in Eunapius' *Lives of the Sophists*?" I queried.

He wasn't impressed. "Even I can do that," he told me. "Not in the mountains on the wild side of Jiwaka, admittedly, but I've been back in the fringes of civilization for a while. I was hoping you might know something more."

"Know?" I countered already having scanned the wikipedia entry. "No, I don't *know* any more—but that doesn't mean that my historical expertise is irrelevant."

"You can read between the lines?"

"Of course."

"And?"

I could have asked him why he wanted to know, although, inevitably I had a strong suspicion, and it didn't really matter. I wanted to show off anyway. If battle was going to be joined, I wanted to show that I had my armor all ready and brightly polished.

"You have to consider the historical context," I said, flicking quickly to the entry on Eunapius, although merely as an *aide memoire*, because I had heard of him. Historians tend to have heard of other historians, even if they've never read them, considering them to be fellow members of the same club. "The fourth century was an era when neoplatonists and other schools of pagan thought were involved in relentless controversies with the pugnacious Christian apologists who were trying to seize the intellectual high ground. Whatever Christian philosophers actually argued, their opponents knew full well that their principal marketing strategy was based on Christ's alleged miracle-working, the supposed proof of his divine warrant. Inevitably, by way of reprisal, the pagan philosophers, as well as Christian heretics in search of a synthesis with pagan thought, like the Gnostics, had begun inventing miracle-workers of their own—Apollonius of Tyana, Simon Magus, and so on—in order to establish rival claims of inspiration and revelation, or at last to cheapen the Christian claim that their figurehead was unique. Eunapius, who was bitterly hostile to Christianity, probably wanted to get in on the game, and wanted to invent his own miracle-worker—so he did. As I say, I don't *know* anything; but Sosipatra the prophetess looks to me like just one more invented carbon-copy counter-christ."

"You're saying that she never existed?"

"I'm saying that if a person of that name did exist, and was a neoplatonist philosopher, she surely wasn't the prophetess and miracle-worker that Eunapius made her out to be."

"Because she couldn't have been—because it's impossible to see through time?"

"Precisely."

"I knew you were going to say that," he observed.

"I know you knew," I told him. "But you asked anyway."

"True," he said. "Just checking. It's been ten years, after all."

"I haven't changed."

"I can tell. I have…but not fundamentally. And I haven't given up—but you knew that, didn't you?"

"I've been working on that assumption."

"And yet you didn't tell me to go away. You let me buy you a cup of coffee, and you let Claire invite me to dinner. Because you're till curious, aren't you? In spite of everything, you can't get rid of that niggling curiosity, that philosophical itch, that faint suspicion that maybe history doesn't have a monopoly, that maybe it really is possible to see time as it really is and not as our craven senses insist on trying to force it to be."

He was right, of course—about me, at least, if not about the nature of time. But what I said was: "You're my oldest friend, the only one remaining from the Golden Age. I'm glad to see you again. But you know as well as I do, on the basis of long experience, that you're not going to convert me, any more than I'm going to convert you. That's always been the very essence of our friendship, hasn't it? Paradoxical as it might be, this really is one of those cases in which opposite poles attract, hardly capable of existing without their opposition. Why else would you have missed me, given that you have such a full and engaging life?"

He smiled. "So you're going to help us out?" he queried.

"If you mean, am I going to disagree with everything you tell me and show me, like the loyal devil's advocate I am," I said, "possibly; but it depends what it is you've got your teeth into—and quite frankly, asking me what I know about Sosipatra of Ephesus doesn't seem to me to be a promising opening gambit. There is one condition that I absolutely insist on imposing, though."

"Which is?"

"That you leave Claire and Melody out of it. Whatever you and I might do, and Christiane, if she's involved, as she obviously is, it stays between the three of us. You do not attempt to involve them."

"I had no intention of doing so. It's your so-called common sense I want, to keep me in check, and at least partially honest. The nature of the exercise demands an objective observer. You've always been mine. There's no one else I trust."

"But if I'm reading between the lines correctly," I said, "you're not playing Jekyll-and-Hyde yourself this time? It's Christiane who's under observation?"

"I never was playing Jekyll-and-Hyde," he told me, "but yes, obviously, Christiane is the primary subject, for the moment, and I don't want to take any further steps until I've had you check her out and I've heard what you have to say about our progress thus far. Afterwards…well, one step at a time."

I hesitated. "Look, Jim," I said, "I'm not entirely happy about lending myself to your messing about with somebody else's mind. It was bad enough when I was party to your messing about with your own, and the last experiment certainly didn't work out well, so far as I could see, but at least you and I were the only ones at risk of harm, and we both had some idea of what we were doing…."

"Christiane knows what she's doing," Jimmy said flatly. "Far better than I do, in fact. Once you've met her…and we ought to be on our way, don't you think?…you'll see what I mean." He got up as he spoke, as if the discussion were concluded, although it certainly wasn't. I followed him meekly to the door, though.

I waited until we were outside and heading down the hill before I said: "Okay. I'm reassured by the fact that she's pushing forty, and that you're not playing Svengali to some poor hapless Trilby, but even if it's an honest *folie-à-deux*, I'm assuming that here's still some kind of psychotropic drug involved, and that you're feeding it to her?"

"Obviously. Nothing illegal, though."

"Obviously not, as it's presumably something you dug up as a result of recent ethnomedical investigations in the wilds of Papua New Guinea—but that's a pure technicality and you know it. If it's a psychotropic, then it's dangerous *ipso facto*. You must see that it creates a problem for me, ethically."

"Crap. You know full well that we're going to do what we're going to do anyway. You're not facilitating anything, or giving it your blessing. All we want from you is what I wanted from you back in the eighties, and again in the nineties and the noughties: a clinical eye that can help us weigh up what we're really dealing with. I won't say that you're the best brake-man in the world, but you're the only one I know...the only one I trust. I didn't come here to beg, though, Mark—I came to offer you an opportunity. I came to offer you a chance to get another glimpse of what lies beyond the narrow horizons of your philosophy. I know it's not something you've ever actively wanted...but you've given in to the temptation before, and you're a man who doesn't change."

"You're going to tell me now that this time, it'll be different, aren't you?"

"Yes, it will. No blades, Mark, I swear. This time, it really is just a matter of perception, of the quest for enlightenment. And this time...."

He left it there, unwilling to say out loud that this time, he really had found the way—because he'd said that before, and he hadn't, and he knew, now, that he hadn't then, and that he really ought not to make any extravagant claims now, until he'd provided the proof.

I was convinced, of course, even before he began to explain, and even before he introduced me to his partner in delusion, that once again, he hadn't found the key, because I was convinced that there was no key to find. But I didn't tell him so, because there was no point...and, to tell the truth, because he was absolutely right. I'm a man who doesn't change. I can't. And I had given into the lure of temptation before, even though it had nearly cast me an eye, not once, but twice, when I really ought to have learned circumspection. So I knew, as we headed down the hill, just as I'd known when I found him lurking in my path outside the school gates, that I was going to give in to the temptation again.

Why?

Not kismet, for sure—but because, when time melts away, it doesn't obliterate the past; it just brings it back again...and perhaps it always will...but that way, madness lies. That's the way you really shouldn't go, although this story has to, because, as it unfolded, that's the way it went.

IV

It was in the autumn of 1995, six years after our simultaneous graduation, that I saw Jimmy again. We'd been in touch in the meantime,
via mail and telephone—we'd even exchanged email addresses, which
still seemed novel at the time, and we were still exchanging Christmas
cards—but we hadn't actually met in the flesh. He knew where I was living, though, and where I was working. I was still single at the time; I had
met Claire, but we weren't yet "an item," let alone married or engaged.
On that occasion, he didn't simply lurk outside the school gate waiting
for me to come out; he phoned me at the flat one evening, like a normal,
civilized human being, and told me that that he would be in London for a
couple of weeks, and wondered if I might be willing to take the train into
town on his first evening, so that we could meet in a restaurant near his
hotel in Paddington, "to have dinner and talk over old times".

I was glad to hear from him, after we'd come to the brink of beginning to lose touch. It seemed to me to be thoroughly good idea—and
so it might have been, if we had only confined ourselves to reminiscing
about the golden three years of our adolescent lives and comparing notes
about what had become of us during the previous half-dozen years. But
we didn't, and perhaps that was as much my fault as his. I thought at the
time that perhaps he might even have kept quiet, and not raised the subject at all if I hadn't done so, in a jocular fashion—but once I had time to
reflect, it became obvious to me that if I hadn't brought it up, he would
have done so before we finished coffee; it was, after all, the top item on
his hidden agenda.

My first impression when we shook hands was that I had fared somewhat better than Jimmy in the interim since graduation, even though I
was a novice teacher not long out of probation while he was already
a cog in the massive wheel of Big Pharma, still tiny for the moment
but loaded with infinite potential by comparison with my strictly limited
horizons. His suit was undoubtedly more expensive than mine, but it
looked older and had obviously been subjected to harder wear. He was
still sturdy and muscular but he had a considerably larger gut and his skin
was beginning to take on the slightly sallow appearance that often results
from continual alcohol abuse. In fact, he was looking considerably worse

than he did when I saw him again eleven years later, in 2006, when years of intensive field work had slimmed him down, toughened him up and decisively interrupted any potential slide into alcoholism—but I didn't know that at the time, and I shouldn't get too far ahead of the pattern I've adopted in telling the story.

I saw him take note of the fact that the scar on my face was still visible, though only just, but neither of us mentioned it.

Inevitably, Jimmy had had a more colorful time by far than I had. His marriage to Vanessa hadn't yet ended in divorce, but his report of it suggested to me that it was already in trouble. He blamed long hours spent in the lab and the relentless pressure of the competitive work environment, but I knew that it wasn't always the lab that was keeping him away from home in the evenings. He had already moved around a fair bit without yet being dispatched to remote corners of the Third World. He'd spent time in America and in Switzerland. His salary was already considerably higher than mine, but his lifestyle and spending patterns were exceeding its scope and he was running up debts, working overtime just to meet interest payments.

The net result of all the differences exposed while catching up with the interim in our lives, it seemed to me, was that, even though I wasn't yet certain that Claire was the wife I wanted, let alone whether she would agree to the proposal if I decided that she was, I was well on the way to my target, contented and safe, while Jimmy was living with the melancholy consciousness of a life that was already threatening to go off the rails, in danger of being wrecked on the viaduct of profligacy.

We'd just reached dessert and hadn't yet ordered coffee, when Jimmy pronounced a summary judgment on everything that we'd discussed during the first two courses. "You haven't changed a bit," he said, with a slight sigh. "You're still the sanest, most down-to-earth person I've ever known."

"Thanks," I said. "I'll take it as a compliment, even though I'm not sure it was meant as one. For what it's worth, you're pretty much the same yourself—still the same recklessness, but still the same charm." I was exaggerating, for the sake of politeness, but it was accurate enough. The same charm was still there, and the same magnetism. The edges had barely been knocked off his optimism, in spite of his difficulties and complaints.

"I'll take it as a compliment too," he said, "even though, etc."

That was when I committed the gaffe. "And at least you've given up the futile attempt to open the doors of perception," I commented.

"What makes you think that?" he countered.

Naively, I was slightly surprised. "Because I thought you'd have mentioned it if you hadn't," I said, honestly.

"I thought we ought to get the trivia out of the way first. Of course I haven't given up. In fact, I'm making good progress."

"In spite of all the pressure on your time, and having a trophy wife to maintain?"

"Yes. A good deal of my work is relevant, because I get a certain amount of choice in the compounds I analyze and the experiments I carry out—the Company makes it a point of principle to encourage initiative and let the tech staff track the bees in their bonnet back to the hive. On top of that, I keep up with my reading and my thinking. I've realized that the matter is more complicated than I thought when I was dropping acid. I thought then that it was a matter of revelation—that once you opened the doors that the garden would be displayed before you in all is floral glory, but it's not like that."

"So what is it like?" I asked, guardedly, knowing that whatever complication he had in mind was unlikely to appeal to my sense of mental discipline."

"You're a historian," he said, "so you know all about Pythagoras, right—the guy with the theorem."

"I know that Pythagoras didn't invent the theorem named after him," I countered. "I also know that the supposed accounts of his life were written hundreds of years after his death, by people with a philosophical agenda, and there probably isn't an ounce of reliable assertion in them."

"Haven't changed a bit," he repeated. "What about the assertion that he remembered having three—or was it four—previous lives?"

"Well," I said, "his followers certainly believed in metempsychosis—it was one of the central planks of his philosophy, and there's plenty of documentation confirming that. They passed it on to Plato, so that neo-Pythagorean philosophy and neo-Platonist philosophy remained intimately entangled for hundreds of years, until the Christians finally stamped them out at the end of the fourth century A.D. Plenty of time for Pythagoras himself to have been reborn a dozen times and more—but oddly enough, hardly anyone seems to have remembered being him. Do you?"

"Not yet," he countered, airily. "What do you think of all the experiments modern hypnotherapists are carrying out in past life regression?"

"Unconvincing, in a word."

"And you're not at all impressed by thousands of years of Hindu and Buddhist belief in serial reincarnation?"

"No."

"The Christians did a good job, then, back in the fourth century, didn't they?"

"I don't believe in Heaven and Hell either. In my book, dead is dead. Consciousness evaporates and the body rots. Nothing remains but the legacy of good and evil deeds, works of art and, for those privileged enough to be repeatedly copied or printed, writings: the substance of history."

"But you would say that, wouldn't you? As a historian, it's in your economic and intellectual interest to claim that everything is contained in your subject, and that nothing needs to be added, except a little bit of hard scientific detail, by way of trimmings."

"I wouldn't go that far," I said, modestly, not at all sure that I wouldn't but not about to admit that I was being guided by vulgar pride in my science rather than the power of imperious reason applied to empirical facts."

"It isn't just the Hindus and the Buddhists, either," he said. "If you set aside the brutal oppressions of Christian colonialism and the Islamic carbon copy, practically every human culture there has ever been has revered its ancestors, and believed that it remains possible to enter into communication with them, either by means of entrancement or the use of some kind of psychotropic aid, or both."

"That's not the same thing as metempsychosis," I pointed out.

"No, but it's related. All such beliefs might well refer to the same hyperreality, of which fugitive glimpses can be caught, one way or another."

"Fugitive being the operative word," I said.

"No," he said, "*hyperreality* being the operative word: the wilderness that lies beyond the prison walls of consciousness, the bunker mentality of positivism. It's not easy to see through the cracks, but the cracks are there, and the light comes through, in bright shafts that make the dust motes of consciousness shine. If you deny that, you're denying the experience of millions of human beings extending over a hundred thousand years. What kind of historian does that?"

By that time, we had finished the coffee. Jimmy had a smudge of cappuccino cream on his upper lip. I was drinking espresso.

Jimmy threw his credit card into the saucer the waiter discreetly placed on the table without even glancing at the carefully-folded bill, signed the slip with equal carelessness and dropped a ten pound note on the table by way of a tip. I let him do it without volunteering to make a contribution.

The flow was broken, though, and the spell almost seemed to have dissipated. Almost.

As we wandered towards the door, Jimmy suddenly said: "Do you ever sit with acid-trippers these days, Mark, to keep them anchored to the real world?"

"Of course not," I told him, feeling the first slight hint of a chill enter the social atmosphere. "There's no call for that sort of thing in the circles I move in." It seemed far more diplomatic than any reference to the possibility of getting hurt, and it was true, after a fashion. Ecstasy and amphetamines were still the drugs of choice in the circles I moved in, although I never touched such stuff myself, let alone cocaine, which seemed to be making steady headway, fashion-wise.

"Would you be interested in providing that kind of service, if anybody wanted it?" he asked, tentatively.

"Why?" I parried, sighing inside. "Do you know someone who does?"

I should simply have said no, flatly and firmly. I don't know to this day why I didn't. Perhaps seeing Jimmy had reminded me that the old, free days had had a lot of fun in them, which had evaporated in the austere atmosphere of the school, and perhaps I was feeling a trifle nostalgic. Perhaps I'd had just enough wine to skew my sense of proportion.

I wasn't in the least surprised when he told me that he might be in quest of some such assistance himself.

"Not acid, mind," he said, without even looking to see what kind of expression might have overtaken my face. "These days, I try to treat my brain chemistry with at least a modicum of the respect it deserves. This is something quite different."

While he walked back to Paddington with me and we waited underneath the indicator for the platform of the next inter-city train to be indicated, Jimmy told me that he'd been experimenting with state-of-the-art biofeedback equipment imported from the States.

"It's great," he said. "I did TM for a while after graduation, and a bit of EST, and a couple of years back I got into computerized neuro-linguistic programming. About the same time, I was taking hypnotherapy to help me give up smoking, and I did the whole self-induced light trance bit. It's all the same stuff, really. The biofeedback kit makes it all much easier because you can watch your own brain waves on the monitors while you train yourself to control them. The elementary tricks are easy—generating the alpha-rhythm, damping down the theta—but you can go a lot further if you have the concentration. Trouble is, you pretty soon learn to trance yourself out so completely that you can't pay attention to yourself any more…and I still suffer from the same old problem. When I wake up, I can't remember a damn thing. I've tried leaving the Dictaphone running, obviously, but I can't remember to keep talking when I drift off. What I need, Mark, is someone reliable to sit with me and ask questions, to make sure I keep feeding the tape."

I remembered the tapes we'd made seven years before, which had presumably gone in the bin, and couldn't help wondering whether his memory had obligingly censored out the awful embarrassment of their utter futility. I wondered, too, whether the painful awareness that his marriage, and his entire adult life, seemed to be heading for a train-wreck had set him off on some lunatic quest to recover his lost youth.

"I don't get it," I said. "What are you trying to achieve by all this self-hypnosis malarkey? What is it that you want me to ask questions *about*? Past lives? You want to regress yourself and go in search of ancestral memories?"

"Exactly," he said, as the platform number finally flicked up, giving me and a couple of hundred other passengers a lousy five minutes to get through the barrier and sprint up the platform to reach the second class carriages.

"I've got to go," I told him.

"I know," he replied, with equanimity. He'd made his point, even though I hadn't actually agreed to anything, in so many words. "I'll ring you tomorrow to fix a time and place, he added."

Then he turned and walked away.

* * * *

As promised, Jimmy rang me the following day, at seven-thirty in the morning, before I set off for school, when I was only just out of the shower and not yet dressed. Obviously, I had deduced by then that the only reason he'd made contact again was to put his proposition, to involve me in his hopeless quest to open a path to what he was apparently now calling "hyperreality." I remember thinking at the time that he was probably making a belated attempt to recover a little of his ruined innocence and squandered potential, and that it was just another fad, like LSD—and, apparently, TM, EST, NLP and God only knew how may other fashionable acronyms.

Maybe, I thought, the best thing to do was help him through it and get it over with, so that he could settle down to the serious job of saving his marriage, if it was still salvageable, and making further progress at work, which was obviously still wide open to enterprise and endeavor.

I thought I still understood him, even after few years of separation. And I took comfort in the fact that when he'd talked about "regression" he was thinking in terms of hypothetical past lives, not UFO abductions, or memories of childhood sex abuse. At least his imaginary hyperreality didn't seem to be frankly insane, or scabrously unsavory; if it was lunacy, it was a relatively decent sort of lunacy, and if he did contrive to conjure up imaginary memories of being Pythagoras, that would probably be a lot more interesting than summoning up impressions of being a midshipman on Nelson's *Victory* or Gladstone's butler, albeit a lot harder for a conscientious historian to check against any kind of documentary record.

I understood, too, that he hadn't called me simply because I had been a witness to his early development, a friend in better times. He thought that there was something he needed to prove to me—something that would supplement his earlier acts of contrition by demonstrating that he hadn't scarred me for life for nothing. He really had talked himself into believing that he was on to something, and he wanted to let me in on it because I'd already paid the price of admission.

I thought, in my still-youthful arrogance, that it was a bit pathetic—a bit tragic, in a way—but it was also rather touching. Or so I thought. That was how I convinced myself that I really ought to do as he asked, not for my own benefit, but for his. I thought—or thought that I thought—that if Jimmy's conscience was still troubling him, then I ought to give him a chance to put it at rest.

Even so, I put up a convincing struggle.

"I don't think that's a good idea, Jimmy," I said, when he told me he wanted me to go up to London for the entire weekend, where he'd contrived to obtain the use of a flat that his employers used to put up visiting scientists and businessmen, even though he wasn't yet at a pay grade that entitled him to such perks. "Quite frankly, I think past life regression is just moonshine. Some of the subjects might be quite innocent, in seriously believing the fantasies they conjure up under the influence of the power of suggestion, but their sincerity doesn't make what they're satisfying any truer. It annoys me somewhat, and, to tell you the truth, it disgusts me a little. If offends my historian's conscience."

As I say, I was still young, even more prone to arrogance at twenty-seven that I had been at twenty-one. Teaching can do that to you if you're not careful, because of the act you have to put on to maintain authority over the kids.

"That's why I need you, Mark," he said, in his breezily flattering fashion. "I need sanity. I need skepticism. I need someone without the slightest tolerance for bullshit of any kind. And it's Jim these days, remember—I shortened it at work, when I felt the need to cultivate a little more *gravitas*, and now I'm Jim to everyone. There was a horrible period, if you recall, when only football pundits, bad comedians and the littlest Osmond were Jimmies, and I allowed myself to keep the handle for far too long."

In the end, as I'd know that I would the night before, I let him talk me into it. I went straight from school to the station on Friday evening and followed the instructions he'd given me to find the flat, which only required a short journey on the Bakerloo line and a five minute walk. Jimmy called up a local pizza-parlor to arrange a delivery so that we wouldn't have to go out.

We ate the pizzas straight from the boxes without the benefit of cutlery. "It saves washing up," Jimmy explained, unnecessarily—but he did condescend to polish a couple of glasses from which to drink the Hungarian Pinot Noir he'd thoughtfully laid in beforehand to accompany the meal.

The "study", where he had installed his biofeedback equipment, was hardly a model of tidiness, even though he'd only been in the flat for a couple of days and would presumably have to leave it in pristine condition when he moved on. One way and another, he seemed to accumulated a lot of paper, although the merest glance and the scattered sheets told me that it was mostly related to his real work, incomprehensible to a non-specialist like myself. Jimmy cleared a handful away from an armchair that looked as if it might have been assembled from an Ikea flatpack so that I could sit down, dumping it into a corner where a sizeable pile was already beginning to grow.

Then he put on something that looked like a wire-mesh skull-cap and stuck his left hand into a black box which allegedly kept track of his pulse, blood-pressure and skin-moisture.

"Not a bad lie-detector if you use it on innocents," he remarked, "but it didn't take long to train myself to take conscious control of the supposedly tell-tale signs. I don't say that I can beat any polygraph in the world now, but I could have a decent stab at it."

I didn't find this information particularly reassuring, in view of the nature of the experiment we were about to conduct. Jimmy showed me the various displays on his electroencephalograph, which was a good deal more complicated than I'd anticipated. He tried to talk me through the significance of the various plots, but most of the science I knew had come from child-friendly books I'd been given as presents in my school-days, in which dinosaurs and amateur astronomy played a more prominent part than the mysteries of the human brain. I nodded wisely when he mentioned alpha-rhythms again, having heard somewhere that they were the conscious brain's resting state, and tried to look as if I understood what he meant by "theta", but he must have caught on to the fact that I was bluffing.

"Well," he said, "you don't actually need to know the technical stuff. The computer keeps track of all the hard data. Your job is to deal with the stuff that requires thought and ingenuity."

He issued me with a list of questions I was supposed to ask him once he'd thoroughly entranced himself. They were utterly innocuous, beginning with "What's your name?" and "What's the date?" and progressing through routine matters of occupation and education to more open-ended enquiries about hopes and fears for the future. When I'd read through them he impressed it upon me that they were only a very rough guide, and that I must feel free to improvise as and when the need arose.

"I know you think it's crazy, Mark," he said, as I arched my eyebrows skeptically, "but even if everything we dredge up is completely false, it'll still be interesting. Even if we regard it as a pure product of the imagination, it'll still require explanation."

"I suppose you have some reason for expecting something bizarre?" I said, in order not to have to comment on that judgment. "You do have some inkling of what you've supposedly remembered during previous dives into your deep psyche?"

"I have flashes," he said, in a somber tone which was presumably intended to make me take him seriously. "Enough to make me curious—but I don't want to put preconceptions into your mind. Anyway, we'll start off gently and leave the deep-psyche diving till you've got used to the procedure. Shall we get on with it?"

I nodded, wearily.

I was a lot wearier when we finished, way past midnight, five exhausting hours later.

Jimmy wanted to listen to the whole thing, but I was far too tired. "I've already heard it, Jim," I pointed out, "and I already know what I think—but I don't want to put any preconceptions into your mind. Let me know what you think when you've heard it. I'm going to bed."

The trouble with audiotape is that it's a real-time medium. What takes five hours to record takes five hours to play back. When I eventually rolled out of bed the next morning, far too early—I can never sleep properly in strange beds—Jimmy still had more than an hour of crap to play back.

I'd already decided that it would be a good idea to go for a brisk walk before Jimmy revealed that he didn't have any milk and hadn't arranged to have a morning paper delivered. A trip to the nearest general store then became an urgent necessity. I didn't hurry back, and when I returned I took all the time I possibly could over breakfast and the *Guardian*. I wasn't looking forward to the conversation that I knew we were going to have.

"Well," said Jimmy, when he'd finished. "It's not what I expected."

"It's not what I expected either," I told him. "Assuming, for the sake of charity, that it's not a wind-up, you appear to be the victim of a depressingly unimaginative subconscious mind."

"What do you mean?" he asked.

I looked at him hard, but it certainly seemed that he really didn't know.

"I know it's out of sequence," I said, "but if you rearrange the bits of the supposed past life that you recounted in such detail, I think you'll find them pathetically familiar."

He hadn't slept at all, and he was looking distinctly bleary-eyed, but even so, he managed to look at me as if I were the crazy one. "Detail is right," he said. "I had no idea that I knew that much about Victorian England. Frankly, I'd prefer to have gone a little further back, but maybe it's best to take things one at a time. If that's the life I led in the nineteenth century, I suppose I'll have to lump it—it's not as if one can choose one's past incarnations, is not?"

"Actually," I said, "if that's your evidence, it seems that one can. As plagiarism goes, though, it's a trifle over-obvious, don't you think?"

"I have no idea what you're talking about, Mark," he said, with blatant honesty.

"The harrowing tale of an illegitimate child of early Victorian times, uncomfortably brought up in the workhouse, unsuccessfully apprenticed, driven to a life of petty crime, forced into the company of murderous scoundrels, ultimately saved by a miracle of coincidence and resorted to his rightful position in a middle-class safe haven—with the customary climactic inheritance and marriage to look forward to, in the longer term. That doesn't seem familiar to you?"

It seemed quite convincing to me," he said, defensively. "There's a lot of detail in it—stuff I'm sure I never knew before—and even though it isn't sequential, you can't possibly say that it's incoherent."

"No," I said, with a slight sigh. "It's not incoherent. Very neat, in fact—as you might expect, considering that it's *Oliver Twist*, practically word for bloody word."

"*Oliver Twist*?" he repeated, skeptically.

"Charles Dickens' most famous novel, with the names changed and a few key episodes diplomatically excised or superficially reworked. No riot caused by asking for second helpings in the workhouse, for instance. I suppose that would have been too much of a dead giveaway even for your subconscious yarn-spinner."

"You're telling me that I spent the best five hours in a trance, telling you the plot of a book?"

"The plot of a book so well-known that even people who've never read it know pretty well how it goes," I pointed out. "Are you really telling me that you didn't recognize it when you played it back? I figured out what was going on by the time we were two hours in, but I let it go on to the end just to see how far you could take it. All the way, obviously."

"No," he said, a trifle foolishly. "I had no idea. I've never read *Oliver Twist*."

"Or seen the movie on TV? Or the Lionel Bart musical with all the cute songs?"

"It's not my sort of thing," he said. "No, I can assure you that I haven't seen any of them. I've never read anything by Dickens, although I've seen Scrooge on TV at Christmas because you can't avoid him."

"But as I said, it's a plot that's so familiar that even people who haven't seen any of its manifestations have to be vaguely familiar with it."

"But what about all the detail?"

"It's not an exact copy, obviously, but there's nothing there that couldn't be improvised on the bare bones of the plot.

He thought about it for a couple of minutes before he hit upon the obvious ploy. "But all the things Dickens was writing about were real, weren't they?" he said. "There really were workhouses, and orphans really did have a lousy time, and there must surely have been criminal gangs."

"There's a theory," I admitted, "that Dickens based the character of Fagin on a real fence by the name of Ikey Solomons"—but you didn't call your gang-master Solomons any more than you called him Fagin."

"But there's nothing impossible in it, or even improbable," he insisted "It could be an account of an actual life, and the fact that it resembles the plot of a Dickens novel might just mean that Dickens was reflecting the reality of his times. Isn't that what novelists usually do?" He really thought that it was. He'd specialized in science at school, at university and in his profession. Much of the supposed non-fiction he read was, in my view, merely dishonest fiction, but he didn't read novels, and never had. He literally had no idea what novels were really like, and how distortive they were as supposed mirrors of their time.

I tried to explain why Oliver Twist wasn't really a documentary about the travails of the London poor in Victorian times. "But it could have been worse, Jim," I reassured him, eventually. "If it had been *A Christmas Carol*, or *Treasure Island*, what would *that* have said about your unconscious mind? If plagiarism is your only hyperreal resource in conjuring up past lives, you can at least be grateful that it elected to model you on an innocent child rather than a haunted miser or a one-legged pirate."

Jimmy refused to take any consolation from that observation. He also refused to be put off by it. He was determined that the experiment should continue. "There must be more," he insisted. "I've never been a great reader, so I can't possibly go on reproducing the story-lines of old books, even if you're right in your assertion that that's what I did last night. It's just a matter of going deeper, of getting down to psychic *terra incognita*, where I'll be forced to discover something real...or at least to make it up from scratch. It's just a matter of going further back in time."

"No it's not," I told him, confidently. "It won't help to tell yourself to go back to Roman times, or even to the wastelands of prehistory. You might never have read specific stories set in those times, but you have a ready-made image of them distilled from movies and history books and TV documentaries: images that have leached into your mind by a kind of intellectual osmosis. You're not really delving into the past, Jimmy. You're just putting together bits and pieces of knowledge, building a kind of jigsaw. Beyond that…well, there are all kinds of other images and ideas you've taken in and domesticated. It doesn't really make much difference whether you build imaginary histories, or sciencefictional tales of alien visitation, or visions of Heaven and Hell. It's all just a pick-and-mix from the cliché factory, because there's nothing else it can be."

He didn't take offense. "You're wrong, Mark," he said, after a pause for dramatic effect. "I *have* gone deeper—much deeper. I never managed to bring much back that my waking memory could grasp for long, but I know there's something there that's richer and stranger than anything you or I ever have read. I'll prove it to you, given time."

"You can't, Jimmy," I told him, dully. "It can't be done. Anything you say in answer to my questions will be explicable in the terms I've just outlined. Anything short of the key to Cosmic Truth, that is—and even that would probably be unrecognizable, if it were even imaginable."

"That's why I need you," he said, with a kind of persistent patience that I couldn't recognize from the old days. "I need you to play devil's advocate. Let's go get some lunch at the local pub. Then I'll take a nap, and when I wake up, I'll be ready to take another turn under the wire."

I knew there was no easy alternative, so I accepted the inevitable with as much grace as I could. I did as I was asked. We had lunch; he took a nap; and then he hooked himself up again.

But he was wrong; he wasn't ready to take another turn. Even with the aid of the biofeedback machine, he couldn't put himself into a trance. He became frustrated—and the more frustrated he became, the more difficult it became to get himself into the altered state of consciousness for which he was aiming. In the end, he had to accept that he needed a proper night's sleep rather than a cat-nap.

"It's my fault," he said, nobly. "We shouldn't have started so late yesterday, and I shouldn't have stayed up afterwards instead of going to bed. I was too impatient. I've been looking forward to this for too long, and when I finally got the chance, I rushed things. And now we've only got one more day, because I can't do next weekend—I've got all this bloody stuff to get through, and meetings every day. You have no idea how relentless it is, Mark. You have a really cushy billet back at your old school."

"It's not as easy as all that," I told him, defensively. "I might not have as much paperwork as this to get through, as yet, but things aren't getting any easier. Time was, so I've heard, when you could just teach, but now you have to record your lesson plans and tick off endless lists of bullet-points to provide hard evidence that you've covered everything in the syllabus, and the Ministry of Education keep changing the goalposts every time they commission a new consultation. Honestly, Jimmy. It's enough to drive a person crazy, if they don't have the discipline and determination to keep on top of it all."

I'd lost him by the time I got to lesson plans. He wasn't interested.

"I need to stay focused," he told me, with unintended irony. "I need to stay conscious. The self-hypnosis isn't enough on its own, and might be a blind alley, if you're right about it never being able to produce anything that qualifies as persuasive evidence. I need *that*." He waved his hand vaguely at the pile of papers that had started growing in the corner, still fairly slim at present, but with obvious potential to become a real wad.

"What are they?" I asked.

"Reams and reams of computer print-out. Stupid, really. We have memory-sticks now, we should carry the data around in electronic form and just plug it into a computer to display it. Laptops will get better and better. Paper's already obsolete—but habits die hard."

"I know that it's computer print-out," I told him, "but of what?"

"Oh, biochemical analyses of dozens of psychotropic cocktails. Have you tried magic mushrooms, by the way?"

"No."

"You should. And the lab-synthesized stuff that you can buy on the black market at present is just the tip of the iceberg. We're literally producing data like that by the ton, with the aid of the new PCR machines, and we can't analyze it fast enough, let alone test the isolated products in any disciplined fashion—but give me five years, or ten at the most, and I'll be able to develop purified hallucinogens, euphorics, soporifics and anything you like, in a disciplined manner, by the score. Somewhere in all that"—again he waved his hand at the ominous pile—"is the key of the door. Somewhere in there is the pathway to revelation, to true perception, to the way out of the prison. And if it isn't in there already, well, I'll bloody well go out and find it, if I have to go to the ends of the earth. Because whatever you might say, people *have* obtained glimpses in the past—thousands of them. They didn't have the right conceptual apparatus to help them understand what they glimpsed, and maybe we don't, either, thanks to two thousand years of Christianity and Islam stamping out even the attempts to understand, but we have the tools if we have the will...or we will have within ten years...twenty at the absolute most. Trust me, Mark—it will come."

I didn't believe a word of it. And the rest of the weekend, it seemed to me, proved me right. We slept on Saturday night, and we hooked Jimmy up to the biofeedback apparatus again on Sunday morning, and he put himself into a trance, and we switched on the apparatus. I followed the script of his questions, amended in such a way as to go deeper and further into time immemorial…and for the best part of five hours, Jimmy produced fragmentary impressions of things seen or felt, which added up to a kaleidoscope of fragments of Arcadia, mundanity and catastrophe, mixed in more or less equal proportions, but in utter and complete confusion. There were no *lives*, as such, just *moments*. There was detail a-plenty, but nothing spectacular, nothing innovative, nothing crucial and, above all, nothing convincing. It was just imagistic confetti.

Jimmy was practically biting his knuckles while he played it back, and seemed more than once to be on the brink of tears.

"Damn it," he said, repeatedly. And in the end: "Next time…."

For him, it wasn't over, by any means, but for me it was. For me, it had failed, and I didn't even have a scar to show for it.

On Sunday evening, I went home. Jimmy didn't call me again during the eight or ten further days that he stayed in London. Shortly thereafter, he sent me a postcard telling me that he was being posted abroad, initially to the States, for an intensive training course that would equip him for expeditions in Central and South America.

That, I suppose, is when his career as a biopirate—or valuable auxiliary of various humanitarian organizations, depending on your point of view—actually achieved lift-off.

I didn't expect to hear from him for some time, and I didn't, except for a couple of picture postcards and a handful of emails, which contained details of his adventures in the jungle—more anecdote than scientific reportage—and nothing at all about metempsychosis. But I knew that he wasn't going to let go of that particular bone, and I already suspected that when he did finally contact me again, in the course of some flying visit to London, in order "to catch up and reminisce about old times," that something would have come out of that ludicrous pile of computer print-out, or some supplement thereto.

That something, I felt sure even in advance, would succeed in convincing the ever-impressionable Jimmy McKinnon that it really was possible for people to make contact with their ancestors in the depths of time, and that doing so would somehow give him the key that he needed to break out of the prison of consciousness, and not only glimpse the hyperreal world but begin to comprehend it, in its infinity and its eternity.

I was right, obviously…but how I wished, when the time actually came, that I'd been wrong.

V

Jimmy's MSF angel was waiting for us on the pavement outside the Premier Inn. She didn't look like an angel, but that was only to be expected. Like him, she was still wearing one of the outfits that she'd worn out in the wilds of Papua New Guinea: trousers and a top somewhat reminiscent of hospital scrubs or army fatigues. She wasn't wearing a hat, though. Her hair was cropped short, as was presumably necessary and eminently practical for a hospital in the tropics, which, especially in combination with the clothing and her slim and wiry figure, gave her a somewhat masculine appearance, even though her sun-bronzed face was pretty enough, given her age.

When she caught sight of Jimmy she smiled and waved to him, but she didn't run to meet him or kiss him when he arrived. Indeed, it was me she greeted, after looking me up and down in an appraising fashion before offering her hand to be shaken.

She didn't seem to be as old as Jimmy had implied; even though her complexion had suffered somewhat from exposure to the tropical sun; I wouldn't have estimated her age at a day over thirty-five. She wasn't very tall—perhaps five-four. She had an attractive sparkle in her eye and a pleasant smile.

"I've had the desk call a taxi," she told Jimmy, before letting go of my hand. "It'll be here in a couple of minutes." Then she turned her attention back to me. "Hi, Mark," she said. "I'm Christiane Sacy. Jim's told me a lot about you."

"You have the advantage of me, then," I said. "I haven't even had the chance to look you up on Facebook."

She laughed. "I'm no more on Facebook than you are," she said. "And if Jim hasn't spent the last twenty minutes talking about how wonderful I am, I'll have difficulty forgiving him."

"We had other things to catch up on," Jimmy put in, swiftly. "It's been a long time, and Mark has a wife and a daughter to tell me about."

"So I understand," she said, smiling at us both in a fashion that implied that she hadn't meant what she'd said about not forgiving Jimmy for not singing her praises. "Your daughter's called Melody? She's eighteen now? I'm looking forward to meeting her—and your wife, of course, as we're in similar lines of business. It's very kind of her to invite us to dinner. I don't know anyone at all in England, I'm afraid, and poor Jim was practically in quarantine for the first week after we landed—they called it having a thorough check-up, but either way, he could hardly stir from St. Thomas's—and after that he had to go through all his old reports with auditors from the Company, going back years, although it's not as if he hasn't kept them properly up to date with the documentation, in some weird urban desert called Basingstoke...so we haven't seen anyone *socially*, as it were, and this will be a real treat for us both. But I'm rambling, forgive me."

"Nothing to forgive," I assured her, thinking that she didn't look like a confidence trickster or a lunatic—but confidence tricksters and lunatics rarely do, at first glance.

The taxi pulled up then, and we piled in. It was a black cab, so there was plenty of room for all three of us in the back.

"I'm not usually so talkative," Christiane continued, once we were under way. "I haven't really readapted to Europe yet. I've been in Indonesia for more than ten years, at Jiwaka for five. I could have come back, of course—my contract guarantees home—but with no one to come back to...well, you just don't get around to it, unless you pick up something nasty, like poor Jim. I guess I have an iron constitution, immune to almost everything on account of having lived in its midst for so long."

"I thought I had an iron constitution too," Jimmy put in, ruefully.

"Not my same, my love," she countered. "I'm exposed to the routine bugs, the ones the locals live with one a day-to-day basis. You actually head off into the untracked wilderness, to look for the tribes that shun their fellows, the misanthropic cultures, and you come into contact with diseases that no one else ever contracts."

"It's a dark and lonely job," said Jim, sarcastically, "but somebody has to do it."

She seemed to be familiar with the Robert Benchley gloss on the quote, because she blushed visibly, in spite of her tan. "But you're a historian, Mark," she said, changing the subject. "What's your period?"

"I'm a schoolteacher," I told her. "We don't have periods any more, just the national curriculum. Once, I had ideas about doing my own research, writing my book, but I never wanted to focus narrowly on a particular slice of time. I was interested in the span of history, the continuity, the major movements, the rise, decline and fall of empires, the kind of ideas that Spengler and Toynbee used to bat around. But all that's very unfashionable nowadays, and it's too big to get any kind of handle on, especially if you're just a part-time hobbyist playing truant from marking. And when you have a family...."

"Yes, of course," she said, but not wistfully. If she regretted the path she'd chosen now that it was too late the turn back, she wasn't about to let it show.

On the other hand, I thought, if she was channeling Sosipatra of Ephesus under the influence of Jimmy's novel psychotropics and the power of his insistent personality, wasn't that symptomatic of a regret of some sort? Once one eliminated the hypothesis that metempsychosis was real and that she really had been Sosipatra in a past life—which was, of course, unthinkable—then one had to look around for a psychological reason for the selection of the fantasy. Maybe that reason was ninety per cent Jimmy, who surely wanted a seeress far more than he wanted yet another lover, but she had to be playing her part in the *folie à deux*. So, from my viewpoint, as the designated brake-man, I had to ask the question: why Sosipatra? What kind of yearning did she represent, from Christiane Sacy's point of view.

The taxi arrived during that pause for thought. It was a short journey, after all; if I'd been alone, or just with Jimmy, I would have walked. I didn't own a car; I'd always walked, except for using trains for long-distance travel, because it was my principal form of exercise; it kept me fit. Jimmy might have said that it was simply because I was one of life's pedestrians, and perhaps he would have been right, but it did keep me fit.

While Jimmy paid the driver I ushered Christiane through the garden gate. Claire had the front door open before we reached it.

Once again, Christiane didn't wait to be introduced, but simply declared herself. Jimmy made some terse comment about how nice it was to see Claire again, and offered Melody a few compliments about how much she'd grown and how lovely she looked. By the time he'd finished eyeing her up and reflexively scoring her in a scale from one to ten—possibly a six—but in a strictly objective and disinterred fashion, Christiane and Claire were already well on the way to becoming sisters in spirit.

It didn't take long for dinner to turn into the Claire and Christine show, mainly because Jimmy and I couldn't talk about the things that were uppermost in our minds, because I had forbidden it and he was respecting my wishes.

Melody was almost as interested in Christiane as Claire was; she hardly spared Jimmy a glance, exactly as one might expect an eighteen-year-old not to do to a man exactly her father's age, but Christiane was something else from her point of view: an exotic creature, and perhaps a potential role-model of sorts.

Claire had always been a good talker, an expert at keeping conversations rolling, and Christiane, in spite of her protests about being utterly unused to civilized company and European social norms, maintained the same loquaciousness of which she'd given signs in the cab, easily working through the gaps when Claire or Melody had to disappear into the kitchen to keep the substance of the dinner flowing. The food was elementary—mushroom soup out of cardboard cartons, with croutons; salmon steaks with relatively humdrum vegetables—but it probably seemed way out of the ordinary to Jimmy and Christiane, and the Australian Shiraz helped it go down nicely, even though it was common-or-garden supermarket stock that had probably been on special offer.

Anyway, everything went very smoothly, it seemed to me, for the first hour and more, and I actually came close to enjoying myself. We didn't often have people to dinner, and when we did it was almost invariably relatives.

"I wish I had your courage," Claire said to Christiane, once she'd informed herself to her own satisfaction with regard to the kind of job her MSF counterpart did and the kind of life she led. "I'm nowhere near the front line, even in the hospital; I hardly ever see patients—just records. The wards might almost be on the far side of the Moon, so for as my everyday routines are concerned. But you're not only in the front line but way ahead of it, a commando in medical no-man's-land."

"Actually," said Christiane," I suspect that there's less difference than you might think, and my description has probably romanticized it somewhat. I'm in the tent, obviously; I can smell the stink, and I have to be prepared to lend a hand with anything; but essentially, I'm an administrator, just as you are. My primary responsibility, officially, at least, is to keep the records straight, to organize shifts, and to act as a go-between."

"Between whom?" Claire asked.

"Between the people—the patients, primarily, but by no means just them, and the doctors. We're allocated local interpreters, of course, whose job is to help negotiate the various language barriers, but that's only part of the problem. The interpreters only know what the words mean and what the people are saying, but in the medical context the problem is much more complicated than that—and that's how I became involved with Jimmy."

"I thought he was just a patient," I put in, although I already knew that they'd known one another for years, well enough to sleep together occasionally.

"He was, of late, and a priority patient—although I'm not supposed to admit that there are hierarchies in the treatment of patients. But he's been far more than that over the years—and I'm not just talking about his work expediting supplies when we run short, and conjuring up equipment…not to mention listing our clients for drug trials, so that they can sometimes get medicines that aren't available in the west yet."

"I'm sure the Company appreciates the supply of human guinea-pigs," I observed, snidely.

Jimmy just raised his eyes to the ceiling but Christiane snapped back.

"Don't be like that, Mark. We're very grateful to take part in the trials, believe me, and so are the patients. He's saved lives—dozens, if not hundreds. And with regard to interpreting, and the help he's given me, specifically, he's been a godsend. What he does and what he knows are far more vital to my kind of work than my employers, or even the doctors, really understand. In a place like Jiwaka, where you have patients trekking in from all directions, sometimes from places where you didn't even know there were places, let alone people, you can't just run down a list of symptoms to check the way you do in a European hospital. You do that as well, of course, but if you're to treat them effectively you need far more information than that.

"Most Europeans think of ethnomedicine as a study of bizarre beliefs, but it's not. Here, you have medicine and you have something you call 'alternatve medicine,' much of which is regarded as mere superstition by its non-adherents, and people who train as homeopaths or experts in aromatherapy are regarded as cranks and confidence tricksters by those outside their own tribe, but that way of thinking can't be applied to the situation we have out in Jiwaka."

"If the local medicines didn't work," Claire put in, "There wouldn't be any point in Mr. McKinnon's job. Presumably, the trick is to figure out which ones do work and which ones don't. Either way, when patients present at your hospital, you need to know what it is they think they've got, and what treatments they've applied of their own accord, before you can make your own diagnoses and plan your own countermeasures."

"That's all true," said Christiane, perhaps a trifle generously, "but the matter is even more complicated than that. You're still representing the situation within a European framework of thought, in which people are assumed to have theories of disease and beliefs about appropriate remedies, and regard treatments in the same way we do. But the tribesmen don't think that way. They don't have theories, and they don't really have beliefs; they have practices, which they don't try to analyze the way we do. Even MSF doctors have a particular way of thinking about disease and treatment that they learned in medical school—and they need that, and it's absolutely right that they have it, but it does have the side-effect that they have great difficult putting themselves in the shoes of their patients, and seeing their predicaments from their point of view.

"Jimmy does understand, because he has to. For him, ethnomedicine isn't just a discipline invented by academics so that westerners can categorize and analyze quaint native beliefs in a patronizing fashion. He's out in the field half the time, figuring out how the plants that the tribesmen use fit into the context of their everyday lives, their routines and ritual practices, before he can take the stuff back to the Company's facility in Port Moresby, or even in Darwin. He had to fall seriously ill in order to be admitted as a patient to the hospital, and that was a personal disaster for him, but it would have been a catastrophe for me, if the medics hadn't pulled him through."

"Assuming that you both get back to the same place when your leave is over," I put in. That was a real damp rag. Christiane's enthusiasm vanished, and I realized that I'd hit a sore spot. She couldn't be certain that MSF wouldn't change her assignment when her leave finished, and she knew that there was a strong possibility that the Company might change Jimmy's. They lived in that kind of society.

I deduced that Christiane's attitude to her sexual relationship with Jimmy wasn't as casual as Jimmy made out, or as he probably assumed.

After a pause, though, Christiane went on: "Well, wherever he's sent, he'll soon be able to help bridge gaps of understanding between doctors and patients, and he'll be a godsend to the doctors in far more ways than getting them medical supplies. His specialist knowledge will even be able to point them in the direction of a local pharmacopeia that could supplement our supplies, and fill in when there are shortages—as there often are in places like Jiwaka, as you can doubtless imagine."

She was practically oozing hero-worship. I could tell that she was impressing Melody.

"You don't see him as a cynical biopirate plundering the treasure-house of Third World wisdom for the benefit of Big Pharma's profits, then?" I suggested, mischievously.

"Absolutely not," she snapped. "Jimmy's work is of immense practical value on the ground, in the war against disease, and if the people above my level in MSF could only realize that, we could make a lot more use of people like him."

"There are no people like me, darling," Jimmy put in, lightly. "There's only me." He turned to look at me. "Told you so," he said. "Side of the angels."

I was prepared to believe that Christiane Sacy was an angel of sorts, but I was yet to be convinced that Jimmy was really on her side, no matter how firmly persuaded she might be. When women pushing forty fall in love, even if it isn't the first time, they tend to fall hard, because they can feel the turbulent rush from the wings of time's wingèd chariot, and they suspect that it might be the last.

Melody obviously thought that Christiane was some sort of angel too, because I could see the gleam of hero-worship igniting in her gaze too. "It must be very rewarding work," she said. "Your parents must be very proud of you."

Christiane smiled, wryly. "I suppose so," she said. "I haven't seen either of them in quite a while."

"Aren't you going to see them while you're in Europe?" Claire asked, curiously.

"I'm not even sure where they are, although I could find out easily enough. We were never a close family. We were never a family at all, really, although my mother and father were trying it out for size, in case it lived up to the advertising. It didn't. They never technically abandoned me, never stinted on financial support and were certainly never cruel; they're good people, fundamentally, but theirs is a lifestyle that isn't conducive to marriage, let alone to having children. There's a sense in which I was an orphan almost from the start—but I don't hold it against them any more. I understand, now. And it's the way the world is going, isn't it Mark?"

"It's the way that a certain sector of the world's population is evolving," I agreed. "The cosmpolites, I suppose you could call them. But the reproduction of society, and the dynamic of progress, depends on the people who do form stable households and bring up children—the settled people…life's pedestrians, not the jet-setters."

"Yes, of course," Jimmy supplied. "I'm surprised you haven't had six, Mark." He was only being sarcastic because he was having difficulty imagining an ordered and routinized person like me surrounded by the chaotic turbulence of six unruly brats. It didn't even occur to him that he might be being insensitive. He didn't know. How could he?

"I couldn't have any more," Claire put in, flatly, and left it at that. And there it would have been left, as Jimmy realized that he'd put his foot in it, and doubtless wanted to pass on swiftly to safer conversational ground. But Melody had not long turned eighteen, and at that age, people are a trifle foolish.

"It's my fault," she said. "I didn't get born right. I caused complications. Maybe I was set on being an only child—subconsciously, obviously. Probably had sibling trouble in a past life."

She was joking, obviously. She had no idea that she was accidentally treading on dangerous ground. Nobody pretended to take it seriously by rushing to reassure her. We all knew that she didn't really blame herself. Or did she? Perhaps it's really true that there are more true words spoken in jest than anyone consciously intends; but you can't start attributing motives of that sort to the unconscious—or, at least, you shouldn't. That way, madness lies.

Claire was quick to try to heal the rift, to paper over the atmospheric crack—perhaps a little too quick. "What are the two you going to do with your leave?" she asked, not aiming the question directly at either Jimmy or Claire. She didn't actually add: "Since neither of you has any family to visit," but the suggestion nevertheless hung there, She knew that Jimmy's parents were dead; they hadn't even hung on until his last visit, having had him at a relatively late age. He too was an only child.

Jimmy, of course, wasn't about to say anything. I'd forbidden him to do so—but I hadn't forbidden Christiane, and neither had he. Even though he might, in theory, have had the authority, and might have felt obliged to pass on my edict, he hadn't had the opportunity.

"Jim and I are conducting some experiments," she said. "We began them in Jiwaka, but we never had time to get into them properly, and as I was telling Mark in the taxi, things were pressured in London and Basingstoke too. We're hoping to find a suitable location hereabouts, now that our time is really our own, so that Mark can help us out."

I was numb, as if from the shock of a blast, because, perhaps naively, I hadn't expected it, but Claire and Melody had no idea that a bomb had just been dropped.

"Really?" said Claire, genuinely interested. "What kind of experiments?"

Jimmy, sticking to his promise, kept quiet. Christiane didn't.

"Have you heard of past life regression?" she asked, with all the angelic innocence in the world.

Of course they had. Who hasn't? But my eyes were on Claire's and I immediately saw her put two and two together. She was a very smart woman, and Melody had already provided an accidental cue. Claire had no idea what had happened ten years before, because I had never told her, and because I'd ordered Jimmy to keep her out of it them and he had—but she know obviously, that *something* had happened, that something had gone wrong between Jimmy and me, and she knew enough about my past relationship with him—specifically, about the scar in my face—to be able to fit the new datum into her jigsaw puzzle and begin to see the picture.

"Really?" Claire said, in a tone of evident fascination while Melody contented herself with leaning forward avidly, neglecting her dessert, in order not to miss a trick.

"Don't say it," said Christiane, blandly. "You wouldn't have thought I was the type. Neither would I—but I've had a strong interest in the tribal cultures of Indonesia for a long time, and their beliefs. As in many other parts of the world, most if not all of the recently-preliterate tribes of Papua New Guinea use various techniques to access alternative states of consciousness, in which they have access to a kind of spirit world, where answers can be sought to problems in the real world, including disease, primarily from ancestral spirits that have privileged access to a different view of time. Jim's been interested in it for a long time too—metempsychosis, that is. We conducted a few experiments before, but I have to admit that his fever sharpened my interest even further. I've heard a lot of delirious rambling in my time, even delirious rambling in English—but Jim's delirium was…unusual."

"You mean he was remembering past lives?" Claire asked, amazed.

"Not exactly…well, perhaps… but it wasn't so much the other voices in which he sometimes spoke that caught my attention. You'd be surprised how often seeming alternative personalities come out during delirium. It was…well, I suppose you could call it theoretically-impregnated visions. He had a lot to say about the nature of time—incoherent, but thought-provoking, and it connected in interesting ways with some of the visions I had during our experiments, and what I know about Jim's."

That was hardly surprising, I thought, given that theirs was a *folie à deux*, in which they were feeding ideas back and forth. Obviously, their altered states of consciousness, whether drug-induced or disease-induced, would have the same themes, and feature the same kinds of conceptual groping.

Melody had been left behind somewhat in terms of her own conceptual groping. "Are you talking about Shamanism and spirit journeys?" he asked, in the slightly embarrassed one of someone who fears that she might be being naive.

"Shamanism is an anthropological construct, designed to help European theorists get a grip on the phenomena in question," Christiane told her, "which inevitably distorts them, but yes, in the broad sense, which applies the term to a universal phenomenon, Shamanism is as good a description as any." She didn't pass judgment on "spirit journeys," perhaps wisely.

"And you're doing experiments attempting to access these *alternative states of consciousness?*" Claire asked, stressing her own preferred terminology, like the good skeptic she was.

"Yes. Jim's been doing it for years, on and off, but they're the kind of experiment which really needs two people, if not three."

Claire was looking at me now. "And Mark has helped him with experiments of that sort before?" she asked.

Christiane looked at Jimmy, but Jimmy's lips were still sealed. "Apparently," she said, a trifle hesitantly. "Not that there's been much opportunity, from what Jim tells me."

"But now you're helping him?" Claire added.

"Yes."

"How, exactly? Hypnotism? Drugs?"

"Both," Christiane supplied. "It's nothing that eastern hypnotherapists haven't been exploring, and even exploiting, for years, although it's obviously fringe medicine. They inevitably extract it from its primary context, though. Jimmy's expertise in ethnomedicine allows him to get a much clear understanding…and also to take advantage of sophisticated analyses of the psychotropic aids that the native practitioners use."

"And you've actually experienced these alternative states of consciousness?" Melody put in, adapting easily enough to the terminology of choice. "That's wonderful."

"It's dangerous," I said, firmly, trying belatedly—far too late—to take control of the conversation. "Even if it's not actually crazy, it's reckless."

"But you're going to do it," my beloved daughter said, who had not even begun to understand what might be happening, and what might have happened in the past. How could she? "And you've done it before?"

"No, I'm not," I said, bluntly. "And no, I haven't." But I couldn't explain. I had no alternative but to look to Jimmy for support, inviting him—practically begging him—to unseal his lips and try to undo the damage that Christiane had done, entirely accidentally.

"Your Dad has always been my brake-man," Jimmy put in, obligingly. "We go way back, to long before you were born, when we used to experiment with LSD at university. As he says, it's reckless and it can be dangerous, but I'm not a complete fool. I've always seen the necessity of having someone on hand who's sober, someone of unshakable sanity and rationality, who can stop things getting out of hand—a sort of designated driver. He's helped me out before. But this time, I swear, there really isn't any danger. I've made progress—a lot of progress—in my equipment and in my understanding. Mark doesn't believe me yet, and doubtless he shouldn't, until he's seen the evidence, but this time, Christiane and I really do have the means, and the understanding."

Melody was looking at me in a fashion that expressed puzzlement—and, far more dangerously, a hint of admiration. "You've never mentioned any of this to me," she said. Her gaze switched to Claire. "Did you know about it, Mum?"

Clair was loyal as well as smart. "Of course," she said, as if it were no big deal, "but it was a long time ago, before my time, let alone yours."

"Not entirely," said Melody. "I've met Mr. McKinnon before. I wasn't very old, it's true, but I remember…"

"That was one of my less successful ventures," Jimmy put in, quickly. "Your father was invaluable as always, but it confirmed his opinion that…well, as he says, I was a trifle reckless."

"But you actually accessed your past lives?" Melody said, pouncing on the nub of the issue.

"I thought I'd accessed one of them, and got a firm grip on it, for once," Jimmy said, "but your Dad was convinced that I was mistaken, and whatever happened, it certainly wasn't as simple as just remembering a life that my soul had lived before, as if it were a kind of spiritual rubber ball bouncing through a sequence of temporary incarnations. Transanimation doesn't work like that."

"What's transanimation?" Claire asked.

"It's the process by which metempsychosis operates," Christiane chipped in. "The fundamental doctrine of reincarnation simply holds that the soul lives multiple lives, without saying exactly how, or how the transitions are accomplished. Theories of transanimation attempt to explore the metaphysical mechanics and the logic of the process, in the context of more elaborate theories of the soul—theories that don't equate it straightforwardly with consciousness, as crude thinking tends to do."

"I thought it was a simple matter of moral judgment," Claire said. "If you lead a good life, you come back as a human again, in order to try to lead an even better one, as a step on the road to sainthood or ultimate bliss. If you lead a bad life, you come back as a jackal, a hyena, a worm or a cockroach, and have to work your way up the ladder again."

"That is one of the cruder ways of looking at it," Jimmy said, "But even in ancient Greece, from Pythagoras to Proclus, philosophers realized that it had to be more complicated than that. The Christians, of course, didn't like the idea at all; they much preferred Heaven and Hell— so they stamped it out, as best they could, thus preventing its further sophistication, and even its investigation. Now, though, intellectual space is opening up again, gradually. The idea of religious heresy has lost its teeth, although we still have to cope with scientific heresy-hunters. They only burn people metaphorically, but that's because they've learned that subtler techniques of inquisition are more effective."

Claire looked at me. "I think he means you, Mark," she observed, lightly.

"That's me," I said, hastening to make a joke of it "The Matthew Hopkins of modern science, running around with my copy of the anti-*Malleus Maleficarum*, ruthlessly persecuting purveyors of old wives' tales, or at least indoctrinating young and vulnerable minds with the poison of reason."

"Actually," said Jimmy, "I didn't mean Mark at all. He might be stubborn in his views, but he doesn't have a closed mind. It's precisely because he's amenable to reason that I've always valued his input so much. I know that if and when I have contrived to open the doors of perception fully, instead of partially, I'll be able to convince Mark of what there is to be seen, because he's an honest man. And when Mark finally tells me that what I've got is pure gold, I'll know that it is."

I was tempted to say: *In your dreams*—but that, of course, was exactly where he was coming from.

Melody wanted to get back to basics. "So who do you remember being in your past lives?" she asked Christiane, bluntly.

"It's not as simple as that," Christian replied, dutifully. "But under the influence of the drug, my soul is able to access, thus far in a limited way, the attributes of a fourth-century seeress named Sosipatra. We're hoping that if we can bring out that identity more fully, along with her abilities, we'll be able to learn a good deal more about the process and logic of transanimation, and hence about the true nature of time."

And pigs might fly, I thought. I was looking hard at Melody, perhaps even staring, willing her to keep her mouth shut. It was a bad move. I was looking and willing in the wrong direction. Unexpectedly, destiny defied a great many assumptions that I'd always taken for granted at a single stroke, and it was Claire who suddenly said: "Can I try it?"

Not even "Can I watch?" or "Can I help?" but straight in at the deep end. Even Melody seemed shocked.

Nobody asked her what she meant. Everybody knew—and I couldn't just howl "No," could I?

Jimmy, at least, made some attempt to be a hero. "It's far too early to involve anyone else," he said. "There's a long experimental path to travel before we'll have enough data regarding Christiane's experiences even for me to try it on myself. We're scientists, and we have proceed methodically. The whole exercise might be reckless, but that's exactly why we need a brake-man. I can't possibly think about broadening the field-trial until I get a reliable endorsement of the value of what I've done so far."

"From Mark?" Claire knew me; she knew exactly how likely it was that he'd ever get that endorsement from me.

"I trust him," was Jimmy's perfectly simple reply.

"He's a history teacher at a grammar school," Claire observed. "The same grammar school that he attended as a pupil. He's never been anywhere else or done anything else, except for three years at university. He's my husband, and the father of my child, and I love him dearly, but for God's sake, Jim, do you really think he's a fit person to pass judgment on an experiment in *transanimation?*"

And there it was: the collapse occasioned by the explosion. The truth, of which I'd always been conscientiously in search, and had always carefully avoided finding: the truth of what Claire really thought of me, love me as she might.

Again, I tried to make light of it, to make it into a joke. "Thanks for the endorsement," I said. "And you're absolutely right, of course."

Christiane's gaze was flicking back and forth around the faces grouped around the table, knowing that she's precipitated something and trying to figure out exactly how awful the crisis was.

"But that's the whole point, Claire," Jimmy said. "Mark is completely down-to-earth, completely steady, and you love him dearly. He's the only person I know—hell, so far as I can tell, the only person is the world—who has actually cracked the problem of how to live a stable, happy and successful life. Even when I first met him, when were both eighteen years old, I could see that he knew what he wanted from life, and how to get it—and what I admired most about him was his refusal to rush, his determination to be patient, not to get sidetracked and not to make a false move. If I've never been side-tracked—although God knows I've made plenty of false moves, from having been in too much of a hurry—I owe that at least partly to Mark's example, and if I'd taken more advantage of it, I'd have avoided several pitfalls along the way. Of all the souls in all the world, there's none whose extensions through the tangled web of time that I'd rather explore than Mark's. Maybe I'll get the chance, if the present project works out—but in the meantime, yes, I do want his judgment and I value it immensely…just as I'm sure you do, in any and all matters."

But the damage was done. He couldn't possibly be sure of that, and nor, any longer, could I.

The crack didn't spread immediately. Claire accepted the correction readily enough. "Well, if I can't try your magic potion yet," she said. "Can I at least watch? Given that I've shared Mark's settled life for the last twenty years, I must be just as qualified to pass judgment as he is, according to your logic."

"It isn't a sideshow," Jimmy said, still playing the hero. "I'm a scientist, not a stage hypnotist. I wouldn't feel at all comfortable inviting people to watch."

When he looked round to make sure that his army was behind him, though—figuratively speaking, of course—it wasn't.

"Oh, I don't mind at all," said Christiane, blithely. "In fact, now that I've met Mark and Claire, "I can see why you thought it would be a good idea to ask for his help, I'm sure that Claire would be equally helpful."

It was on the tip of Melody's tongue to say: "And me!" or something similar, but I was willing her with every ounce of my utterly impotent will-power not to do it. The effort can't have made any difference, but either she thought about it wisely or didn't have the nerve. She kept quiet—for the time being.

Things had got out of hand—but in all honesty, what could I have done about it? At what point could I have intervened, and how, to steer the ship away from the reef? Admittedly, I hadn't had to phone Claire from the café on Mount Pleasant. I could have made arrangements with Jimmy to meet him in secret, to keep the whole affair under wraps and simply pleaded that I'd been delayed at school when I eventually got home—it was certainly plausible and by no means without precedent—but Claire would have known that something was going on, and how could I have kept it from her, even for a matter of days, without risking a rift of an equally damaging kind?

There was no alternative to but to try make the best of things.

Perhaps, I told myself, it wouldn't be so bad. Perhaps it wouldn't be bad at all. Perhaps Claire would see through the sham, whatever sort of sham it was and simply dismiss it as something unworthy, after all, of her interest. She was a smart woman. She would surely take my side, even if she didn't think of it as "taking my side." The momentary rift would heal; our bond would be confirmed. And Jimmy wouldn't seduce her, and it would surely never enter her head to try to seduce him.

Everything, I told myself, would be all right.

I met Jimmy's eyes, and knew that we both felt the inevitability. I left it to him to say it, though; I was too much of a coward.

"If Christiane doesn't mind," he said, "then I guess there's no objection. The Human Resources people at Basingstoke are trying to find some kind of short-term accommodation in the area—the Company has all kinds of resources hereabouts, now that the Thames Valley is England's answer to Silicon Valley, so it shouldn't be difficult. With luck, I'll be able get something set up by the weekend."

Claire wasn't ready to volunteer our home as an experimental site, because of Melody, although I was perfectly certain that Melody wouldn't have raised any objection, so she just nodded. "Let me know when," was all she said. "I'll do my damnedest to avoid getting caught up at work."

Perhaps for the first time in my life, I blessed the octopoid tentacles of NHS bureaucracy, and prayed that some kind of crisis might develop at the hospital that might tie her up for all the hours that God supplied for at least a week.

But if I was on the side of the angels, they didn't seem to be on mine.

VI

It was eleven years after the biofeedback fiasco, give or take a couple of months, before I saw Jimmy in the flesh again. That was the day he turned up at the school gate, lying in wait for me. "I did actually phone the school," he said, holding up his mobile by way of demonstration, "but I got some snotty secretary saying that she couldn't contact you because you were teaching, and that I couldn't be allowed on the premises to wait for you indoors. Would you believe it?"

I knew the school secretary, and her junior staff, so I had no difficulty at all believing it, and wasn't in the least surprised that no message had reached me telling me that someone had called. I smiled in sympathy.

"It's good to see you, Jimmy. "Welcome to twenty-first century England. You could have phoned a little sooner, if only to let me know that you were back in England. You're looking very fit and well, and I love the hat. Where have you come from? Peru? The Congo?"

"Brazil. Landed at Heathrow three days ago, but the bastards sent a car to pick me up and whisk me away to bloody Stevenage. I haven't had a moment to myself since—literally. At least they let me have a car, so I could drive over here as soon as they let me out of the gate. The parking round here's appalling, by the way, and I haven't seen a pub anywhere."

"If you're driving," I said sanctimoniously, "You shouldn't be drinking. And there aren't any in the immediate neighborhood."

"Well, I need a drink," he said, "even if it's only the one. The car's round the corner. Just give me directions."

I hesitated, but wasn't in any rush to get home. Claire would be at the hospital until five, at least, and Melody, in consequence, would have gone home from school with her friend Jasmine, and wouldn't care what time she was picked up, poor kid.

"Just a quick one," I said. "I've got an eight-year-old latch-key kid to think about. The teaching day might end at four, but responsibility is never-ending."

I gave him directions to the Roebuck, which would have been my local if I were the kind of person who had "a local." At any rate, it was conveniently placed for me to pick up Melody from Jasmine's if Claire didn't get there before me, and whisk her home in time for tea.

Jim ordered himself a pint of real ale, even though that would probably put him over the limit for driving, but I settled for a half of draught cider. To tell the truth, I'd rather have had a glass of wine, but the Roebuck was a trifle old-fashioned, and took a perverse pride in not being a wine-bar. It didn't survive the financial crisis, but that was still a couple of years away back in 2006.

For half an hour we went through the usual rigmarole of catching up, but I did almost all the talking, because I had Claire and Melody to talk about, and he only had Julie, and his second impending divorce, which was not something about which he wanted to wax lyrical. Because time was of the essence, he was in a hurry to fix up an appointment for the real purpose of his visit.

"This time," he assured me, "it will work. I told you ten years ago that I'd find the lever, and I have. It took a little longer than I'd hoped, but I've got it."

"A drug?" I queried. "A psychotropic?"

"Exactly. *The* psychotropic, refined and perfected. It's safe—it's been thoroughly tested on animals, chimps as well as rats and pigs. Believe me, I've done my homework. I've already taken it myself half a dozen times, but you know the problem—you still remember the last time. I'm gradually getting used to it, but even with the Dictaphone, I can't get a good enough record of the experience, because I need someone to ask the right questions—to lead the witness. The Company is letting me use a cottage near Knebworth for a few weeks, while I'm organizing the lab work here to pick up where I left off in Manaos and assemble a team for the clinical trials. It's intensive, but I'm sure I can jig my schedule to fit with yours. I've already cleared Saturday and Sunday, so if you can spare the time from your cozy family life, I'll show you something that you'll never forget—something that will blow your mind."

"It's very short notice, Jim," I protested, feebly.

"That's the pace of life nowadays," he told me. "Anyway, I presume you're going to introduce me to your wife before I have to dash back, so I'll sweet-talk her into letting you come out to play. Is she pretty, by the way?"

"Jim," I said, "I'm forty years old and a bit, and so are you. We're not teenagers on the pull any more. Claire's thirty-five, and yes, she's lovely, but she's not your type, if my memory serves me right."

"I'm a moderately respectable married man myself," he said. "It's just an innocent question. You have nothing to fear from me, even if she can't help finding me devilishly attractive or having romantic illusions about my lifestyle. I envy you your settled life, and wouldn't want to disturb it for the world—so I'll leave the sweet talk entirely to you. But the issue remains: can you get away to play this weekend?"

"I don't have a car."

"I'll come over and pick you up. You can stay overnight at the cottage, and if you don't think it's safe for me to drive you home on Sunday, you can get a taxi to Stevenage station and take the train. But you have to come. I need you—and this, believe me, is the payload. This is the breakthrough. It's the opportunity of a lifetime, for you as well as me."

I didn't believe a word of it, of course, but what alternative did I have? I'd started, back in the eighties, and had continued in the nineties. In a sense, I'd already committed myself, even if it had been eleven years since I'd last seen him.

So I did as he asked. I took him with me to pick Melody up, and just about had time to introduce him to Claire when she got home from the hospital before he had to, as he put it, "dash"—but it was time enough for him to impress her, and to bulldoze her into agreeing that of course he could take me away for a day or two at the weekend, so that we could "have a long chat about old times and renew our friendship."

And that was what we did, at least while we were in the car driving to Knebworth. I had spent the previous couple of days half-hoping that some crisis would crop up at the hospital that would require me to stay at home with Melody, and half-dreading that it might, but in the event, none did, and when I insisted to Claire that all she had to do was pick up the phone, and I'd already be on my way back pronto, she assured me that spending a little "quality time" with Melody would be a joy for her, and that she didn't mind at all how late I got back on Sunday.

Once we had reached, the cottage, however, Jimmy was anxious to get down to business. He had his biofeedback apparatus already set up—a recognizable variant of the previous kit, but shinier and loaded with more powerful electronics, as was only to be expected after ten years of rapid progress. This time, however, Jimmy went a safe fitted into the wall—an honest-to-God safe with a combination lock—before hitching himself up to his ridiculous paraphernalia.

I expected to see a hypodermic syringe, but what he actually took out was merely a yellow-stained sugar lump, that looked rather quaint even by comparison with the tabs of acid we'd dropped twenty years before. He showed it to me with an odd mixture of sheepishness and pride. My heart sank slightly as I looked at it, and for the first time in many self-conscious years I thought I could actually feel the line drawn down my face, from my eye to my chin.

It was psychosomatic, of course, but I couldn't help feeling that the scar had somehow woken up.

"It's much better than acid," he assured me, "and safer too. I've proven that, as I told you. I've calculated the dose perfectly. I don't want to run the risk of disappointing you. You've come a long way."

"What is it?" I asked, a trifle stonily.

"Its chemical name wouldn't mean anything to you," he said, "especially as we've only just made it up, but it's an alkaloid derivative of ayahuasca."

I had always prided myself on my general knowledge, but the name wasn't familiar to me. "What's ayahuasca?" I asked, as if I were playing straight man again, feeding him a cue.

"You might have heard of it as yagé. It's one of the most powerful and longest-established entheogens."

Obviously, I was an even straighter man than I'd imagined. "And what's an entheogen?"

"It means 'engendering the divine within,' apparently—my Greek and Latin aren't good enough to be sure. It's a jargon term used to refer to psychotropic substances used in a religious context for the facilitation of spirit journeys. It's compounded out of leaves from various plants, including species of *Banisyeriopsis* and *Psychotria*—but that's just more jargon. The point is that it's brewed and used throughout the Andean states—Venezuela, Ecuador, Bolivia and Peru—as well as Brazil. Ayahuasca itself mean 'vine of the soul' in Quechua. The principal active compound was once called telepathine, and later harmaline. It was even patented back in the eighties.

"Some twentieth-century movements of a kind you'd probably dismiss as left-over hippies took it up in the context of a syncretic philosophy fusing native and Christian beliefs. It got more than enough publicity then to put it right at the top of Big Pharma's hit list of substances for possible exploitation, and that was what I was sent to Brazil to do: to investigate all the plants of the relevant genera that were used in the brewing process by various tribesmen, to isolate all the psychoactive compounds and examine them one by one to map their effects.

"It's exhausting work, as you can imagine, but the fundamental neurology has progressed by leaps and bounds. Ethics Committees have inevitably held back human testing, even in Brazil, but up the jungle… well, there's no need to go into all that. To cut a long story short, there are more interesting compounds in the mix than harmaline, even before we started tweaking them in order to refine and enhance their active effects. And now…this. I haven't given it a name yet, deliberately.

"Officially, the bosses are only interested in potential medical uses way beyond the purgative effect for which native medicine tended to employ it—horribly messy, but very effective in clearing out gut parasites—but they've never made the slightest attempt to inhibit my investigation of psychotropic effects. Naturally, I've never mentioned metempsychosis even in my unofficial reports, let alone my official ones; I operate on a strictly need to know basis, just as they do."

"Right," I said. "And you've taken the stuff before, how many times?"

"Half a dozen, as I told you—well, maybe ten—but very carefully, in graduated doses, as a conscientious scientist should. Enough, at any rate, to be sure of the effect."

"You've remembered past lives?"

"Well, yes and no. The continuity between lives is more complicated than the old Pythagorean jargon implied—and the later neo-Pythagoreans and neo-Platonists had sophisticated it considerably before the Christians put an end to their research. Proclus and Plotinus certainly get closer to a real sense of the process, and probably the Gnostics too, although very few of their documents seem to have survived—you'd know more about that than I would, and are probably capable of getting more out of it if you bother to investigate. I'm more interested in now and tomorrow than the intuitions of a few ancient Greeks.

"Anyway, it's not a matter of the soul being a kind of spiritual rubber ball that bounces from one body to another, taking on different identities each time, which can occasionally remember their previous versions. The soul is much bigger than that, and much more elastic in the way it stretches through time. Individual bundles of consciousness are, in a sense, more like co-existent multiple personalities within a psychic whole, which are normally closed off and unaware of one another, but can sometimes open up and become aware, and on occasion, overlap and even fuse. You have to bear in mind that your stubborn linear perception of time as a straight line is an illusion forced by the nature of your sensory perception. Seen from a hyperreal viewpoint, time is a unity in which everything is co-existent. So, when one of the multiple personalities that the soul produces is enabled to become aware of others that seem to the imprisoned consciousness to be displaced along the linear continuum, what's happening isn't really analogous to remembering something forgotten. Does that make sense?"

"Not to me," I told him, bluntly.

"Well, it will when you've had time to investigate it properly and analyze it conscientiously. You'll probably be able to make more sense of it than I can, in fact. I'm more interested in the practicality than the theory."

While I was shaking my head at the stupidity of it all, he put the sugar-lump in his mouth and washed it down with the dregs of a nine-tenths-empty bottle of cheap Scotch. Then he hitched himself up to his skullcap and his unreliable lie-detector and closed his eyes.

I didn't say anything more, and he didn't make the slightest attempt to carry the conversation forward. He seemed to be composing himself—putting himself into an allegedly hypnotic trance.

Suddenly, I became convinced that "seemed" was the operative word, and that all of it was just a show, a pretence, some kind of weird joke. Perhaps, I thought, Jimmy wasn't trying to complete his interrupted penance at all. Perhaps he was trying to pay me back in some other, weirder, way. Perhaps he thought I'd made too much fuss of a cut on my face, putting a premature damper on his experiments with acid. Perhaps the accounts of our lives that we'd exchanged in the Roebuck had made him jealous of the fact that mine was such a safe and stable life, while his was on the skids for the second time around. Perhaps, on the other hand, the depression concomitant to his impending second divorce had unhinged him a little more, and made him so fiercely nostalgic for old times that he was desperate to recapture something he'd long let go: the friendship that had bound him temporarily to me, whose firmness had ultimately been sealed in blood.

Perhaps…but it was all futile conjecture, all fantasy pushed up from nowhere by my own overactive subconscious.

After a while, Jimmy seemed to have gone to sleep, but I knew that he hadn't. I knew that whatever else his condition was, it was certainly deceptive and untrustworthy. I looked carefully around, hoping to reassure myself that there was nothing sharp around, but in the usual mess that he always managed to contrive, even in places where he's only been resident for a couple of days, it was difficult to be certain.

I watched the curves making their stately way across the screens on Jimmy's biofeedback monitor, half-convincing myself that I could see the theta track dying down and the long, slow alpha-rhythms taking control of Jimmy's addled brain—and I waited, for what must have been nearly half an hour, until the broad curves of the alpha began to break up and his general neural activity became more fervent again.

I wasn't in any hurry. I switched on the voice-recorder, but I hadn't yet picked up my questionnaire script when Jimmy began to speak.

"*Cogito*," said a voice somewhat deeper than the one he usually used, "*ergo sum*." I couldn't judge the quality of his pronunciation, but I'd read enough popular philosophy to know that "There is a thought, therefore there must be a thinker" is supposed by some scholars to be a better way of starting off the argument than "I think, therefore I am."

"So who are you supposed to be now, Jim?" I asked him, sarcastically, "René Descartes, or the malicious demon of the First Meditation?"

"Who are you?" asked the deeper voice. It sounded surprised, as if it had not expected to be overheard.

"It's only me—Mark," I assured him. "What's *your* name now?"

"Mark Two," I thought the voice said—although it might actually have said: "Mark too."

"Mark who?" I asked, thinking about the old stand-up comedy routine about the man with the hoodoo, and still feeling like a straight man.

"Why not? It'll do as well as any. Only Mark. Mark me. Make my mark. Up to the mark. Full marks, Mark. That's better. I'm getting my bearings now."

"Cunning move, Jim," I remarked. "Failure of the imagination disguised as semi-enigmatic wordplay. Won't wash, though. What year is it, Mark Two?"

"Don't know. Ask me another."

"Where do you live?"

"In here, of course. With Jimmy—but Jimmy don't know and what he don't know won't hurt him. Another."

If I was surprised by that it was only by the fact that Jimmy was calling himself "Jimmy," given that I'd addressed him with the preferred "Jim." I still hadn't picked up the script, and I couldn't remember what came next. I figured that it was time to take advantage of my license to improvise. Even if the game had gone sour, it had still to be played. If I were to have the piss taken out of me, the least I could do was take a little back.

"So what you're telling me, Mark Two" I said, "is that you're some kind of *alter ego*—a fugitive secondary individual within the multiple personality that is Jimmy McKinnon?"

"Bugger off," said the voice that seemed to be trying hard, if rather absurdly, to convince me that it wasn't Jimmy's. "You're leading the witness, arsehole. Ask me a proper question."

"Bugger off yourself, Jim," I said. "I've got better things to do. Just cut the bullshit, will you, and tell me the essential Cosmic Truth. It'll save us both a lot of time."

"Okay," said the voice. "No problem. Neural tissue doesn't regenerate, but neither does it die. You get a dozen livers in the course of a lifetime but only one brain. You probably think that it's the permanent decay of synaptic connections that creates the preferred pathways in the brain providing the electrical foundation of the personality, but you're wrong. Bodily, we're etched by death, because death is the lens that focuses the potential ubiquity of Everyman into the precise definition of the individual face, but the brain doesn't shrivel. We live in parallel with our other potential selves—not just the ones you can read about in books or hear about in petty folklore, but the ones that are stranger than you imagine and stranger than you can imagine. You might think you're hot shit, Not-the-Only Mark, but you're just looking after the flesh while it recovers its destiny, its *habitability*. You're just a waste by-product of reiterative evolution, and that's probably why you're such an arsehole. Now—ask me a hard one."

"Why?" I said, reflexively.

"That's better. Because it helps, of course. It helps me pull myself together, to figure myself out, to calculate my dimensions. So, are you going to help me or not? If so, ask some intelligent questions. If not, send for someone who can."

I was very glad that I'd got all that on tape, because I was certain that I wouldn't have been able to remember it all. What on earth had Jimmy been reading, I wondered? And why was he shoveling it all on to me, consciously or subconsciously, in these tortured circumstances? Why on Earth had I volunteered for this? Why had I even condescended to listen to him when he showed up at the school after ten years with hardly a postcard? How had I contrived to forget that this was the imbecile who'd nearly put my eye out and come within an inch of slicing into my carotid artery? How had I let nostalgia blind me to the fact that Jimmy McKinnon was a dangerous madman, whether he was drugged to the eyeballs or not?

"That's it, is it, Jim?" I said, sarcastically. "That's all we get for our fifty pee? We're just waste-products of evolution, keeping the species ticking over until our true selves can emerge from the recesses of our brains to claim a fleshy heritage worth waiting for? Is that what you're trying to tell me?"

"Well, pardon me," the voice retorted, "I forgot you were a school-teacher. Quite frankly, Mark Not-quite-One, I'm not much interested in debating the issue. What I want you to do is ask me a question worth answering."

"Why should I?" I said. It might have been clever if I'd planned it, but again, it just popped out.

"I already told you," said the voice that was sounding less like Jimmy's by the minute. It was impossible to tell whether its apparent impatience was sincere or ironic. "The reason is that if you don't, neither of us will learn anything, and time is pressing. Jimmy might be able to go on for hours on end while he's straight, but not when he's under the influence. I need the questions Jimmy doesn't ask, Mark, because he doesn't have the right education. Maybe you don't either, but you seem to be all I've got, for now, so you could at least *try*. If you only knew how badly I need those questions…" He left it there.

He was right, of course, whoever and whatever he was; if I couldn't find some better questions, neither of us was going to learn anything.

"How many of you are in there?" I asked, interested in the tale in spite of myself. "How many potential selves does Jimmy have, lurking like the ghosts of the unborn in his unused synaptic pathways?"

"Legion," came the answer, "but the pathways aren't unused, arse-hole. Just because the usage doesn't show up in Jimmy's pathetic excuse for a consciousness, it doesn't mean that they aren't busy. Don't think for a moment that we only come out at night, or when Jimmy's in one of his helpful little trances. That's when we can borrow his spare capacity and turn his various aspects to our own purposes, but we're always around in some form. We have our own good fights to fight, our own contests of the will. How could it be otherwise? Don't think you're any different, my darling. Even dryasdust schoolteachers dream, and if they think their unconscious is under control just because they have a nice wife and a nice kid and a life as dull as ditchwater, they're seriously in denial. You can edit out the others and commit yourself to solitary confinement for life, but you can't kill their source. Believe me, my good friend, you have no idea of the true magnitude of your soul, and its complexity, let alone the direction of its evolution. Even in your tiny brain…and believe be, by comparison with those elsewhen in the web, it really is teeny-weeny, there's far more going on than you'll ever be able to grasp. God, that's better. I'm beginning to get a real feel of myself now. Maybe you're not such an arsehole after all. Ask me another, old pal."

"What's the cube root of ninety-four?" I said. I had a calculator in my jacket pocket. I could have checked the answer later, if he'd deigned to answer.

"Oh, bugger off," he said. "You've just got through to the fount of all fucking wisdom and you want to test it with mental fucking arithmetic? What kind of friend are you? Don't answer that—just ask me a question worth answering."

I couldn't help feeling offended. For two pins I could have got seriously angry. Why, after all, should I play his game? What was in it for me, at the end of the day, but pseudointellectul gibberish?

"What's the true value of Hubble's constant?" I countered.

"What the hell does it matter to you what the true value of Hubble's so-called constant is, history teacher?" the voice came back, seemingly tortured by frustration and disgust. "Your day will be done before your so-called astronomers can devise an accurate yardstick. Judging by the prion precursors in your glia, you'll be lucky if your consciousness lasts until your heart and lungs pack up, Mark One—I wouldn't lay any bets on living much beyond seventy if I were you—so the apparent expansion of the universe and the convolutions of the fabric of space due to the topology of dark matter really don't have any relevance at all to you, and not that much more to me. Ask me another."

I frowned. Obviously, it had been a mistake to ask questions about physics, when I knew full well that I wouldn't be able to understand any answer that was more complicated than a mere number.

"Did Richard III order the murder of the princes in the tower?" I asked.

"Yes. And please don't ask me who Jack the Ripper was, or what happened to the gold of the Incas. Our time is limited, believe me, unless you care to feed me another sugar lump—but better not. This ridiculously feeble body might not be able take the side-effects. We're in what might be called a tight spot here, and the closer we get to the enlightening flame, the greater the danger is that we'll be burned. If I had an ounce of moral fiber, Mark One, I'd probably advise you to leave this business alone, but I can see deep enough into your psyche and deep enough into your future to know that it isn't going to happen. You're hooked, old son, and there's no way back. You go on to the end."

"Not if I don't want to," I told him, irritated by his insulting attitude.

"I didn't say you will, pal, I said you do. There is no destiny, but there's no freedom either. You are what you are, and the more I think about it, alas, so am I. Your friend Jimmy really has no idea what he's doing does he, poor lamb? What makes him think that if he really did manage to get a glimpse of the web of time, he'd be able to survive it? Even he must have figured out by now that there are reasons why consciousness seeks solitary confinement, and why the sane are so desperate to cover over the cracks. You can't save him, Mark. I can see how much you'd like to, but you can't. Save yourself, and those you love. That's all anyone can even try to do. Shit, now I'm getting maudlin. Of all the universes to get stuck in, I have to find myself in one that has a moral order. Do you suppose that here's any other kind? Now there's a question…except, the age of irony being what it is, I don't know the fucking answer, do I? And it wouldn't do me any fucking good if it did would it? I mean, when you get right down to it, existence is a bummer, isn't it, even if the soul is eternal and the cycle of eternity runs to trillions of trillions of years, through the ultimate Gordian knot. It's getting better, is it, sideways if not endways? Well, bully for you, God, but it's no fucking good to me, and even less to you, old pal. Do you want some good advice, Mark One?"

"Have you got any?" I countered, with all the sarcasm I could muster. I really didn't like this incarnation of Jimmy at all, and not just because he wasn't paying any heed to the rigorous zero-tolerance policy on swearing that I had to apply at school.

"Oh yes," he said. "I've got good advice you wouldn't believe."

That, I believed.

"What is it, then?" I asked him.

"Erase this recording. Tell Jim he didn't say a word. Just go home, Mark."

"I can't do that," I told him.

"You can and you do," he said. "Like I said, no destiny, but no freedom. Bugger of a world. But we have to play our part, don't we? Nothing else we can do. So ask me a question, Mark One, and for fuck's sake try to find one that will help me get out of this filthy black mood, if that pea-brain of yours can stretch to an atom of common sense."

For a moment, there, I had almost begin to think that he might have something worthwhile to say, but I realized that he was just some way-ward fragment of Jimmy's unconscious that he normally had the decency to repress, which the ayahuasca had liberated. I'd had enough.

"No," I said. "No more questions. If you have something to say, you can say it. If not, bugger off yourself. I was sick of this stupid game before it even started, and now I'm really sick of it. I don't want to play any more."

Privately, I was telling myself ever more insistently that I should have never have come, that I ought to have known better, that I was a perfect fool for thinking—if only for a moment—that Jimmy McKinnon might have wanted to put things right, to make it up to me, finally to earn the forgiveness I'd been so quick to offer in my youth. In retrospect, looking back a distance, I'm not entirely sure why I was seething with anger, but I was.

"You don't win, Mark," the voice informed me, coldly. "You never win if you won't play, and as you can't opt out you really should make more effort—but you don't. You lose. You lose, Mark Not-even-One. Jimmy won't like it. You're not making any friends here."

"I have enough friends," I told him, flatly. "I've got by for the best part of twenty years without you, Jimmy, and I'll get by easily enough for thirty more. I need friends like you like I need a hole in the head."

"Joke," said the voice, tersely. "You can't see it, but maybe Jimmy will. In fact, you can probably depend on it."

"It's Jim nowadays," I told the voice. "Jimmy got devalued. It's Jim."

"I know him better that you do, Mark One," the voice retorted. "I know what really happened with that scalpel."

"What the hell is that supposed to mean?" I asked—but perversity being what it is, Jim's little joker had decided that it no longer wanted to be asked another, or anything at all. It fell silent.

Jimmy looked for all the world as if he were asleep, but I couldn't read the curves unfolding on the ECG's numerous dials. From alpha to theta, or alpha to omega, it was all Greek to me.

Joke.

"I'm getting out of here, Jim," I told my ex-friend, softly, not really caring whether he or any of his alter egos was listening or not. "I'm go-ing home." But I didn't move—not immediately. I remembered what Mark Two had said about my being able to go home, and his prediction that I would, and I wanted to demonstrate that I had a choice in the mat-ter…if, in fact, I did.

Jimmy didn't wake up for another hour, but he never said another word in any kind of voice. I watched the lines twitching and swaying on the ECG screens for a little while longer, but I couldn't make any sense of them at all. Maybe Jimmy was dreaming and maybe he wasn't—but he certainly wasn't in any fit state to respond to external cues.

The anger died down, but not the impatience. In the end, I gave in. I decided to let Mark Two have the satisfaction. After all, I had a wife and daughter that I loved dearly, and with whom I'd far rather spend time than some foul-mouthed and abusive alter ego of a so-called friend I hadn't seen in eleven years.

During the fifteen or twenty minutes before he finally woke up, I called a cab and picked up the overnight bags I'd never bothered to un-pack. I waited just long enough to say goodbye, but I left before he'd even started playing back the tape.

"You can't go," he said, plaintively—but he was still dazed from the after-effects of the drug.

"I'm sorry, Jim," I said. "This was a mistake. You'll understand when you've played the tape."

* * * *

Perhaps he did understand, and perhaps he didn't. Probably not. At any rate, he didn't call that night, or the next morning. For a day or two, I thought he might not—but when I got home from school on Tuesday night, after a two-hour club supervision session, he was there, chatting to Claire and playing with Melody. They all seemed to be getting on famously.

"Hello, Mark," he said. "I know I should have called, but I didn't know you were going to be late."

I let the blatant non-sequitur pass without comment. With Claire there, and Melody, and no idea what he might have said to them in how-ever long he'd been waiting, I had no idea what to say, and my mouth somehow formed the words: "That's all right," without any real intention on my part.

He returned to Claire. "Do you mind if I borrow him for a little while? I need to ask him a favor, I'll send him back to you in half a hour or so, but we didn't really get as much chance to catch up at the weekend as I would have liked because he was missing the two of you so much, and I'll be going away again shortly, so...." He left the sentence dan-gling, although what he might plausibly have added, I had no idea. He still seemed to me to be speaking entirely in non-sequiturs. But he still had that fatal charm, and it was obvious he'd already won Claire over, one way or another, and Melody too.

"That's all right," Claire said. "Take all the time you need. After all, it might be another ten years before he sees you again, mightn't it?" She was joking. Many a true word....

"Come on," said Jimmy, addressing me again. "I'll buy you a pint in the Roebuck. I really do need to talk to you."

Claire and Melody were both looking on. What could I say? What could I do? I followed him, meekly.

Out of curiosity, I had looked up ayahuasca on the website of the company for whom Jimmy worked, which made no secret of the fact that it was a subject of ongoing interest. The brief note, which had presumably been written by the PR department rather than the scientists working on the project, reported that it was extracted from a South American vine, that it was used by Asaninca shamans as a source of inspirational visions, that its principal active ingredient had been isolated and patented in 1986 by a California-based corporation, but that some twenty other compounds associated with the traditional concoction were under "active investigation." A couple had been licensed for testing, but had not put into commercial production thereafter, because they "appeared to have no immediate curative value"—which meant, I assumed, that they were a solution without a problem, an answer without a question, a treatment without a disease.

Jimmy bought himself a pint of ale, even though he was intending to drive back to Knebworth. I settled for cider again.

"I expect you're wondering why I didn't call on Sunday," he said, when we'd ensconced ourselves on either side of a table in a booth whose red-plush upholstery had seen far better days. I inferred that he was wondering why I hadn't called, to apologize, or at least to explain—but I wasn't in an apologetic mood.

"I presumed that you were embarrassed about wasting my time," I lied.

"I thought we were friends, Mark," he said, quietly. "Was it really necessary to get so upset about a little bad language and vulgar abuse. You knew, didn't you, that it really wasn't me who was talking? You could tell, couldn't you, that it really was another individual, an authentic past life?"

He honestly seemed to believe it—not only that what he was saying was true, but that I ought to know that it was true, that it ought to be as obvious to me as it apparently was to him.

"It was you, Jim," I said. "The voice of your unconscious, I'll grant, rather than anything you'd say to my face while in control of yourself— but it was *you*. So aren't I the one who ought to be saying that I thought we were friends? Aren't I the one who should feel let down?"

He looked at me with his dark and soulful eyes. All the old charm was still there. "Well," he said, after a pause, "I'm sorry that you feel that way, Mark, and if you're right, I can only apologize. If it was me, I honestly wasn't myself, at the time—if that makes any sense."

It didn't, but I knew what he meant.

"You really ought to give it up, Jim," I told him. "You must know that, deep down. If you don't, you'll do yourself some serious harm, mentally if not physically. You heard the tape. Whether you admit that it was you, or keep insisting that it was some past or future self that you were somehow evoking from the depths of time, the danger is clear. The voice as good as admitted it. If you go on, you really will go mad."

"Come on, Mark," he said. "Even you, narrow-minded as you sometimes pretend to be, must have realized that it wasn't nonsense—and it certainly wasn't a hoax. You must have realized that it was something real, something ominous. I have too much trust in your judgment to think otherwise. I know that you ran because you were scared, and I can understand why. But it you hadn't known that it was real, you wouldn't have been scared, and you wouldn't have run. So you know, don't you, that even if it was confused, and unnecessarily foul-mouthed, that it was an actual communication through time—that I really have opened a door, that I really do have an opportunity."

"I'm truly sorry, Jim," but that's not what I heard at all. And I'm sorry, now that I didn't stay, and didn't call you that evening, because I really ought to have done everything I could, there and then, or as soon as possible, to make you see reason. Because you're right: we're friends. I owe you that."

He nodded in satisfaction, but what he said was: "No, you don't owe me anything. I owe you more consideration. It's not fair, turning up the way I did and just expecting you to drop anything in order to help me out in research for which you have no sympathy. You don't owe me anything at all, and I was just presuming on your generosity. But I really did need you, and I do. I need to get in touch with that…whatever it was…again, but I need you there, Mark. I need you to ask the questions. I know that the…let's call it a gremlin, shall we…accused you of not asking the right questions, and mocked the ones you did ask, but the point is that you did ask them, you did provide the stimulation it needed to loosen up and start talking. It was confused, I know, but it wasn't incoherent and it certainly wasn't devoid of meaning, Next time, you'll be ready for it; you won't get scared again. Next time, you'll be able to get it to say more. Even on Saturday, in spite of all the problems, you very nearly got it to calm down, to stop being ratty, and talk to you like a human being, We're *this* close, Mark, and next time…"

I felt that I really ought to stop him.

"There isn't going to be a next time, Jim," I told him. "I refused to be a party to your committing suicide back in eighty-eight, and I won't do it now. You have to stop taking that stuff, Jim, before it kills you or drives you completely off your rocker."

He took a long swig of his pint, thought about it for a moment or two, and then returned to the attack.

"I see where you're coming from Mark. I understand that you're trying to be a friend, the best way you can. But you need to listen to the tape again, in a calmer frame of mind. You need to listen carefully, and analyze it minutely. And then, when you've begun to get a handle on what we're dealing with, we need to do another run. Just one, if you're really that frightened, but we do have to do one more. We're *so close*."

What can you do, when your friend is going insane? It's obvious, of course, what you should do, what you need to do, but what *can* you do? What can you do that can have the effect you want to have, the effect you need to have. Humor him? Not in this instance, for sure. Be cruel to be kind? Maybe—but how? What could I actually do that wouldn't appear to him to be a betrayal of his trust—that wouldn't veritably be a betrayal of his trust?

I didn't know. I didn't know then, and I still don't.

"The reason you asked for my help, Jim," I reminded him, "is that I'm your brake-man. That's my job. I was there on Saturday to be skeptical, to be hard-headed, to be stubbornly reasonable. Did you ever find out what the cube root of ninety-four is, by the way?"

"You did a good job, Mark," he said, soberly. "You really drew him out. He was doped, of course—the ayahuasca released all his normal inhibitions—but it was your prompting that laid the matter bare and got it all on tape, and gave me something to work on. I'm truly grateful for that."

"You're welcome," I told him, guardedly. "But the time really has come to apply the brake, Jim, and I'm applying it. You might not like me for it, and you might think of it as a betrayal of our friendship, but in time, I think, you'll come to see that I'm right. That stuff is too dangerous. Didn't the gremlin say so himself? He didn't say much that was clear, but he did warn you that that you're heading for disaster if you carry on. Unconsciously, you see, Jim, you know that. You know that you have to stop."

He took another swig of ale. I suppressed the temptation to check my wristwatch in a significant fashion, although I was only half way through my half of cider. I'd never lost the habit I'd acquired at university of making drinks last, of spinning them out. Jimmy didn't seem to have retained it, though. His glass was almost empty.

"You know," he said, "We have these fabulous programs at work now. They map the hypothetical biochemistry of all kinds of organic molecules. You always have to test the conclusions on actual flesh in the end, but it's marvelous how much you can get out of theory, by way of pointing out new possibilities and warning about possible side-effects. Trouble is, I was never much of a theorist. I was always a shoot-'em-up-and-see-what-happens kind of guy. There's a school of thought, I know, that says that metempsychosis and all its associated ideas are best left to philosophers and the efforts of cogitation—but that's not my way, Mark. I can't work like that. And I have faith in Nature, you know? I just can't help thinking that, no matter how clever the programs become, they can only extrapolate the premises that are put into them. They can never produce anything really new; they can't think outside the box. But there are still surprises waiting for us out there in the wilderness…molecules we've never even begun to imagine. We'll never find them if we don't go and look, and we'll never really know what they can do until we actually shoot-'em-up and see what happens."

"Maybe so, Jim," I said. "But it's only a matter of time before that approach gets you killed. "If that's who you are, then I guess you have to be content with who you are—but that doesn't mean that you can't be prudent. And if you can be content with who you are, why go looking for people you aren't, in the wilderness of if?"

"Very neat, Mark," he said. "And you're right—that's why I always come back to you, when the crunch comes, when I need a brake-man. But you can't just stamp on the brake—you have to press it slowly if you want to come to a smooth halt. One more time, Mark. One more time can't hurt…and if you want, I'll promise you that it will be the last. After all, you can't deny, can you, that the experiment succeeded? I mean, take away the swearing and the gratuitous insults, and it really was an interesting communication, wasn't it? Plenty of food for thought."

"No, Jim," I said. "Oliver Twist was harmless, but this isn't. I'm sorry if you think I'm letting you down, but I can't."

"Okay," he said. "It's too soon, I can see that. Trouble is, I really don't have long. When John Company calls, we hirelings have to salute and follow orders. I'm their man in Brazil now, their ace, and while the Amazon is top of their to-do list, they won't want me kicking my heels in Blighty…and I have a sneaking suspicion that if Africa moved to the head of their queue, I'd hardly have time to plant my boots on English soil before I was rubbing shoulders with gorillas. I get leave, obviously, but nobody takes it—that's just not the way the system works, unless you contract green monkey virus or get stung by a scorpion the size of a lobster. There's only a narrow window of opportunity, Mark. If you want me to beg, I'll beg, but I need your help. There really is no one else I can trust…if my bosses got wind of it…well, let's not go into that. Need to know. And what I need to know is whether I can rely on you. Name your time and place—your house, if you like…no, I can see that you don't like that idea. Knebworth, then. Just one more trip. An evening, if you can't spare a weekend."

He was drunk, but I knew that it couldn't be just a single pint of strong ale that had achieved that end. It was synergy. The alcohol was interacting with the ayahuasca residues. He was losing it. I began to feel anxious.

I drained my glass and looked at my watch, ostentatiously.

"No, Jim," I said. "I can't. I really can't."

"Too busy," he said, regretfully. "I knew, really, but I had to try. I've beaten him, you know. He thought he had all the advantages, but once I knew enough about him, partly thanks to you—what he was and how he operated—I knew what I had to do. I had the biofeedback equipment, you see. It was just a matter of training myself to take control of systems that usually operate subconsciously. I'm in control now."

I felt a sudden chill, as I realized that the synergistic reaction between the after-effects off his damned psychotropic and the real ale were getting visibly worse. Thanks to "care in the community," it was no longer a rare experience to find oneself talking to someone who seemed sane at first, and then became anything but, without even a hint of transition. The papers were always reporting cases in which unmedicated schizophrenics flipped out and stabbed someone to death with a kitchen knife. It was practically a sign of the times.

"It was just a hallucination, Jim," I said to him, in a soothing tone. "It was just a drug-induced dream. You don't really have a Mr. Hyde lurking behind your Jekyllesque consciousness."

"We all do, Mark," he said, earnestly. "That's exactly the point. Your consciousness—your self, as you like to call it—is only one of the patterns latent in the synaptic labyrinth of your brain. There are others. You glimpse them sometimes, in dreams and nightmares, but mostly they're invisible and inaudible. They watch, and they wait."

"Wait for what?" I asked, unable to resist being drawn in.

"For their time. You know, of course, that ours isn't a first-generation star, and that the Earth and its ecosphere are assembled out of building-blocks produced by a long-gone supernova?"

"I've read popular astronomy books," I admitted.

"Of course you have. Well, ours isn't a second-generation system either. Some of its material is the debris of a long-gone ecosphere—debris that still contains seeds of life, replete with evolutionary potential. Evolution isn't a matter of chance, Mark. Natural selection really is a process of selection. The whole process is recapitulative, heading towards an ultimate goal. Human intelligence is just a step on the way—a test-program, intended to develop the capacities of the wetware while its ultimate inheritors are still in the making. They're in there, Mark. They watch us, and learn from us. Our role is to ask the questions to which they'll eventually provide the answers, to wear in the shoes into which they'll eventually step."

I had read a few popular psychology books, and I thought I'd read enough to recognize a classic schizophrenic delusion when I was confronted by one.

"It's not true, Jimmy," I said, very softly. "It's all made up. If I'd thought for a minute that you'd spend the next five or ten years trying to elaborate the nonsense you put on that tape, I'd…"

I stopped because I had a sudden attack of honesty. What would I have done, even if I'd known that? Nothing. What could I do. Nothing— except, perhaps, to refuse to meet him when he finally got around to calling me, having brought his delusion to some kind of pitch of perfection.

"I can prove it to you, Mark," he said mildly. "I promised you that, didn't I? Well, I can't let you go this time without showing you. You see, the inheritors have powers we don't. Their minds can do things ours can't—or couldn't, until I started using the biofeedback apparatus and the ayahuasca derivative to take control of the real powers invested in my brain."

"What powers, Jimmy?" I asked, feeling more pity than scorn, but neither outweighing curiosity in determining my tone.

That, of course, was when he took the knife out of the inner pocket of his coat. It was still in the strong polystyrene packet in which it had hung on the peg in some hardware shop, so I knew that it would be sharp—maybe not as sharp as the old scalpel, but sharp enough. It wasn't an ostentatious carving knife, just one of those little black-handled kitchen-knives like the one that Claire used for peeling potatoes and slicing tomatoes: a "kitchen devil," I believe they're called.

Oddly enough, there was no chill. I'd been there. I'd done that.

So that's is what this is all about, I thought. *A replay. A reiteration. We did the rehearsal twenty years ago, and now it's time for the actual performance.*

"I won't do it, Jimmy," I said, coldly. "I won't stop you. This time, if you want to, you can cut a hole in your head to let the spirituality in and the common sense out. I won't stop you, Jimmy. Not again. I just can't."

"Don't be stupid, Mark," he said, wearily. "I'm not going to cut a hole in my head. I just want to show you something."

He took off his jacket and set it down beside him on the cushion of the booth, without bothering to transfer the wallet to his trousers. Then he began to roll up his left sleeve.

I began to look around the crowded pub, to see if anybody else was paying attention. A couple at the bar immediately turned to look into one another's eyes, so I knew that we weren't unobserved—but I also knew that if anything ugly developed, no one would come to my assistance.

It was the twenty-first century after all; there could be twenty or thirty people within easy range, but all they'd do was watch. They wouldn't get involved. People didn't—not any more.

When he'd exposed his arm all the way to the elbow, with his shirt-sleeve neatly rolled, Jimmy took the kitchen devil out of its plastic wrapping.

"Don't, Jimmy," I said. "Please don't." But I sat perfectly still. There was no way I was going to try to take the knife off him.

The background sound seemed slightly hushed, as if half a dozen conversations were being put on hold while ten or fifteen people watched us out of the corners of their eyes, but it might have been an illusion caused by my own brain's reflexive withdrawal from its own stream of consciousness.

Jimmy placed the point of the blade in the crook of his elbow and ran it down the whole length of his inner arm until its further progress was interrupted by the buckle on his watch-strap.

Blood flooded out. I'd read that the only efficient ways to commit suicide with a knife are to cut your own throat or to cut your arm later-ally, deep enough to open a long slit in the artery. I have no idea whether Jimmy cut deep enough to slit the artery, but for a second—or maybe two—there was certainly no shortage of bright red blood. It covered his entire arm, spreading out both ways like a river in flood.

And then it stopped.

The flood seemed to hesitate, as if it had changed its mind.

Then the blood just turned around, and flowed back into the crease in Jimmy's pale flesh. The crease itself disappeared, as the flesh sealed itself shut and resumed its former state.

I could imagine the surreptitious onlookers thinking that Jimmy must be some kind of an illusionist, and that it was a hell of a trick, but I knew that I'd seen what I'd seen. I knew that I could trust my eyes.

I also knew that it didn't prove a thing. It was remarkable, but it didn't prove a thing. Madmen can do strange things.

"You see," Jimmy said, smugly. "It isn't going to be as easy as they thought. We don't have to let them take over, Mark. We can keep it all for ourselves, if only we have the will to fight—and the wit. I can save the world for humankind, Mark. I know how to do it, and I can teach everyone else. I can make myself immortal, Mark—and you can be immortal too."

I just sat there, staring at him. The noise of surrounding conversations grew again, retaining its normal volume—but the barflies were still watching us from the corners of their eyes, just in case Jimmy had another trick even better than the last.

Jimmy rolled his sleeve back down again, but he didn't put his jacket on. I wanted to remind him that it wasn't safe to leave his wallet there, that he ought to keep it on his person, but I was speechless. He left the knife on the table, neatly positioned on a coaster. There was no trace of blood on the blade.

Jimmy picked up his empty glass, and asked me if I wanted another.

"I'll get you a lemonade," I murmured, glad of the excuse to get up. "You can't have any more alcohol. You're driving."

The ruck at the bar wasn't bad, but it still took a couple of minutes to get served, and the interval probably seemed a lot longer than it actually was before I picked up the half-pint of lemonade and the half-pint of cider and carried them carefully back to the booth, where Jimmy was waiting. He'd put his jacket on again.

Or so it appeared—until he spoke.

"I expect you're wondering why I haven't called," he said—except that this time, he wasn't using his own voice. He was using the other voice: the deeper one; the one that had demanded that I ask it more interesting questions.

"That's not funny, Jim," I said. "It really isn't."

"This is Mark," said the voice. "Mark Twain. *The Mysterious Stranger*." When I didn't say anything, it added: "Joke."

But Jimmy didn't read fiction. He had never heard of *The Mysterious Stranger*. Or had he? Sometimes we pick up these odd items of data in passing, without even being consciously aware of it.

"I'm really not in the mood for jokes, Jim," I said. "I know you're still partly drugged, by the residues of that stuff you take, but I know that you're not really some kind of Dr. Jekyll character who's lost the ability to hide his Mr. Hyde, so why don't we just let it alone and have a quiet drink, and a sensible conversation about old times?"

"You're such a bore, Mark One," the voice said. "Imagine the tedious time your inner self must have had all these years. Now Jimmy, for all his faults, was always interesting."

"Was?" I queried.

"You didn't actually think that I was going to let him save the world for humankind, do you? I mean, it was interesting to let him think he'd taken control, because he asked such lovely questions, but it's gone far enough, don't you think? Pulling tricks like the last one is fine in private, and it doesn't cut much ice in a smoky pub on a wet weekday evening, but this guy has contacts. People who know his work take him seriously. Tonight was a step too far, Mark One. I know you're harmless, but you're only the beginning. This was just a test. Tomorrow, or next week…you do understand, don't you, why I can't allow that to happen?"

I understood, or thought I did. Jimmy had watched me sit perfectly still while he'd slit his arm, so he was going to try me again. This time, he was going to go all the way, just as he'd done when the acid first addled his brain.

"It doesn't make sense, Jim," I told him, wearily. "It never did. The someone else you're pretending to be can't threaten to kill you, because he'd die too. It's stupid."

"You should have asked better questions, Mark Two," the voice told me, contemptuously. "If you had, you'd know that my kind don't work that way. I can come back, Mark Two. I can keep on and on coming back, until the time is right. You're mortal. So is Jimmy, in spite of his new parlor tricks. We're not. We're the elect, Mark Two: the climax community of all flesh."

It still didn't make sense, and I resented the contempt. I wasn't going to take it.

"I'm not going to stop you, Jim," I said. "I'm not even going to try. I've taken enough scars from you. You could have cost me an eye, or cut the artery in my neck. Never again, Jim. Not now, not ever."

I meant every word. It was the sane and reasonable thing to say, just as it was the sane and reasonable thing to do.

Jimmy picked up the knife and aimed the blade at his right eye.

He was threatening to plunge the four-inch blade into the pupil and through the lens and the retina, then through the bone at the back of the orbit and into the brain.

Four inches wasn't very much, but I knew that it would be enough. I knew how small an eyeball is. I'd seen diagrams.

As soon as his hand twitched, I moved. I just couldn't help myself. I hurled myself across the table and grabbed his wrist with both hands, hauling it backwards and down with all my strength.

Jimmy had grower old, but he hadn't lost his strength. I was no longer as slender as I had been at nineteen, but the weight I'd put on wasn't muscle. If anything, I was at a greater disdavantage at forty than I'd been at nineteen. Even so, I fought his arm down on to the table and I went on fighting.

In the end, I forced him to let go of the knife. The cider spilled, but the lemonade didn't.

I thought at first that I hadn't hurt myself at all, but when a drop of blood fell from my face like a tear into the rivulet of cider that had spilled from my fallen glass I touched my cheek with my free hand. I found that he'd somehow contrived to open a tiny cut half way up or down my old scar. It was trivial, though; I knew that it wouldn't cause me any difficulty.

Nobody came to my aid, although there must have been a moment when virtually every eye in that section of the bar had turned to watch us. As soon as it was obvious that I had custody of the knife, and that Jimmy wasn't fighting any more, every one of those curious eyes had swiveled away, pretending to be deeply engrossed in its own affairs.

"Never again, Jimmy," I said, harshly. "Never. Don't call me again. Whatever it is, the answer's no."

I walked out of the pub, glad that my cider had spilled so I didn't have to leave it standing there, the way people in movies always do when their scene ends. I looked back once from the doorway. Jimmy was looking right at me, with a smile on his face. As our eyes met his lips formed the word "joke", but there was no sound to tell me which voice was behind the gesture.

I threw the knife into a rubbish bin on the street corner.

When I got home, Claire noticed the tiny cut immediately, but I told her that it was nothing and she accepted that judgment as the final word. She didn't ask about Jimmy; she just took it for granted that he'd "had to dash" back to Knebworth, as he'd told her he would.

He didn't call, but I got a postcard from Brazil a couple of months late.

Glad to be back, it read. *Feel a lot better now, entirely my old self again. See you next time I'm in Blighty.*

In your dreams, arsehole, I thought.

I meant it. But I didn't mean it forever. As time melts away, it often takes ill-feeling with it.

VII

When Jimmy and Christiane set off back to the Premier Inn—again traveling by taxi, although the distance was easily walkable, it was after eleven, and Claire and I both had to work the next day, but simply going to bed and getting a good night' sleep was apparently not on the agenda—except for Melody, of course, who was still not quite old enough not to be packed off to bed on parental command. Ours was a well-organized household, where we didn't have rows—not, at any rate, over silly things like that.

"We shouldn't leave it too late," I reminded Claire. "We've both got heavy days tomorrow." Actually I didn't, but I knew that she did, and felt that I ought to show solidarity.

"Contractually," she said, "neither of us has to be in before nine; it's just our conscientious habits that make us go in early. I'll probably have to be at work until six or seven anyhow, and going in at the crack of dawn would be overdoing it, so we have an hour to spare, at least, and we still have to do the washing up."

It was odd arithmetic, but Claire had a way with numbers that came with being in hospital admin, where bare-faced lying with the aid of spurious calculations was and essential component of the art.

"Why didn't you tell me that you'd helped Jim McKinnon with occult experiments before?" Claire asked me, once Melody had been dismissed and I had my hands deep in the washing-up bowl. She had a tea towel in her hand, ready to dry the dishes as soon as I had rinsed them and put them in the rack, and obviously had no intention of leaving me to do the job on my own.

"I told you about the scar I got at uni," I reminded her.

"Yes you did," she conceded, "but you never told me what happened ten years ago, or about the other time he referred to, before we got married. Why not?"

"Because nothing came of it," I told her, although I felt uncomfortable about the partial dishonesty. "It was just a series of wild goose chases. This one will be no different. He might have talked that poor girl into believing that she's a reincarnation of some ancient seeress, and got her to feed their mutual delusion while supposedly under hypnosis and the effect of some exotic drug, but it's all just imagination, the stuff of dreams."

Naturally, she plucked out the key phrase effortlessly. "Poor girl?" she queried. "She's thirty-five if she's a day, and she struck me as being thoroughly *compos mentis*. You can't do a job like hers without a great deal of discipline—believe me, I know. I've never been to Jaywacker, or wherever they were, and I don't have a smattering of half a dozen tribal languages, so I have no idea what conditions she was working under or exactly what problems she faced day in and day out, but that only increases my respect for her. She's nobody's fool."

"I don't say that she is," I countered, "but she's obviously fallen for Jimmy hard, as many women have in the past, and she's direly anxious to please him. She's feeding his obsession. I don't say that she's doing it cynically, and she might well have persuaded herself to believe it, but once you eliminate the impossible—and her being a reincarnation of Sosipatra of Ephesus definitely belongs in that category—what you have left is where you have to search for the truth. One way or another, they're stringing one another along, and deep down, they know it—but they need me to convince them of the fact. So they'll do their damnedest to string me along too, and it isn't until I refuse to be strung that they might—just might—condescend to let go. The fact that there are two of them this time complicates the issue, though."

"And you think it'll complicate the issue even further if there are two of us? Especially if they manage to string me along too—because you don't trust me to form a mature and rational judgment."

"Of course I do," I lied, although I wasn't sure entirely why I didn't trust her to see through the bullshit, if not right away, then eventually. Perhaps I was simply frightened. After all, I had heard what she really thought about my never having been anywhere and never having done anything, and having no qualification at all to sit in judgment on an experiment in transanimation.

"So why didn't you want me to get involved?" she demanded.

"You asked if you could try the drug!" I objected. "An untested, unknown psychotropic! Of course I don't want you taking a risk like that. Would you have wanted me to volunteer?"

"I wouldn't have stopped you if you had—although, bearing in mind what you just said about eliminating the impossible, there's no point in even thinking about that hypothesis, is there? But you don't want me involved at all, do you. You want to keep me out of it, just as you did ten years ago, when you wouldn't tell me what caused you to fall out with him, and still won't."

I did my best to avoid the issue, as best I could. "Jimmy and I go back a long way," I said. "I was there when he first started this obsession, and every time he contacts me, it's to drag me into it again. It's difficult for me to say no to him, but dragging someone else into it with me is a step too far, which I don't want to take, partly because it's ridiculous, and partly because I'm mortally afraid that Jimmy is going to take it too far one day and hurt himself, or somebody else. I don't want that to be him, or me, and certainly not you. As he says, he's given me a kind of license to put a brake on him and haul him back when he gets too close to the edge, and I feel obliged to do that for him—but not to ask anyone else to get involved."

"You haven't asked me. Quite the reverse, in fact."

"I haven't forbidden you either," I pointed out.

"Only because you couldn't," she observed, shrewdly, "and you knew that it would have the opposite effect if you tried."

"Perhaps I should have told you what happened last time," I admitted. "It would explain why I don't want you involved this time. For all his charm, Jimmy simply isn't reliable. The scalpel incident wasn't the only time I've had to take a knife out of his hand."

"That's how you got that cut you had when you came back from the pub that time—the pub you've steadfastly refused to set foot in ever since?"

"Yes," I admitted.

"But you didn't tell me because you didn't want to worry me?"

"Yes."

"But now you *do* want to worry me, because you want to put me off any involvement in Jim's experiments?"

I hesitated, but there was no point in denying it. "Yes," I said.

"Even though you're involved yourself, you want to exclude me?"

A simple *yes* no longer seemed adequate, even though it was the long and the short of it. "It's dangerous," I said. "It was bad enough when he was only messing with his own mind in order to try to get some kind of magical glance into a world beyond normal consciousness, but now he's involving others. You can't blame me for wanting to protect you…and Mel."

That seemed to me to be a sound argumentative move. She might have felt slightly insulted that I wanted to shield her, given that she was a mature adult capable of making her own judgments and decisions, but she had to understand my motives, given that she couldn't be entirely separate, in my life and my thinking, from our daughter.

I expected her to demand a full and detailed account of the last experiment, the 2006 experiment, and an explanation of why it had alarmed me so much, and I was ready to give her one now, in order to try to explain how the alternative consciousness that Jimmy had briefly acquired or generated under the influence of his accused drug was so nasty and so crazy, but she didn't.

Our time was limited. I'd already washed the last of the dishes and had automatically moved on to stacking them neatly in the cupboards as she finished wiping them dry. We ought to have been moving in the direction of the bathroom, which would involve a necessary separation before we went to bed—but instead, Claire set about making us both a cup of cocoa. She didn't ask whether I wanted one, she just made the decision and did it. She heated the milk in he microwave, with her usual expertise, achieving the right degree of heating without it boiling over. In the meantime, she planned the continuation of the inquisition.

"What's transanimation?" she demanded.

"The imagined process of metempsychosis," I repeated, almost automatically—but she's already heard the simple definition. I knew that she wanted more than that and I could hardly deny that I'd researched it, to the extent that it could be researched.

"We only have a handful of documents to rely on, from Plato to the various commentators and extrapolators of his work," I went on, "and figuring out their intended meaning isn't straightforward, but the general idea is that the creator of the universe—the demiurge, the cosmic engineer, the cosmic mind, or God—made both matter and souls, souls being the animating principle of living matter. Souls are imagined to exist in two states: one free and unlimited, celestial or luminous souls; the other imprisoned in units of matter, human or animal souls. Souls are immortal by definition, and material beings temporary, so the souls that animate particular bodies have necessarily existed before, in previous incarnations, and perhaps in the unlimited state too—but what it might be possible for the imprisoned mind to remember about previous incarnations or periods of disincarnation is, of necessity, very limited. Apparent glimpses can be achieved while dreaming, but such glimpses are prone to almost instant forgetfulness: hence, an awkward problem for philosophers attempting to understand the situation.

"Most of the ancient philosophers who tried to grapple with the problem were convinced that the cosmic engineer had to be reasonable, perhaps even reason itself, and good, perhaps even good itself—but that instantly raises the problems of why, in that case, irrationality and evil exist, and where individual human souls fit into the picture, apparently being trapped between reason and unreason, good and evil, as they try to plot their course through conscious life. As you said yourself during dinner, most people trying to rationalize the idea have pictured the soul as being on some kind of moral journey, which determines a sequential pattern of incarnations, moving up or down a kind of ladder in which animal incarnations are demotions, while some kind of promotion is possible, at least within, and perhaps from, the human condition.

"The fundamental problem of why irrationality and evil exist at all is tackled in various different ways, some of them ingenious. Proclus, for instance, suggests that in order for the universe to be good, seen from a cosmic viewpoint, it has to be complete; everything that can exist has to exist. Thus, there have to be animals, including predators, and in order to supply those animals with the kind of souls they need to have, there have to be degraded human beings. Thus, although human evil and ir-rationality, seen individually, are perversions of the good and the rational ends at which we ought to be aiming in our lives, its existence is a cosmic necessity, and hence, in some ultimate sense, good.

"Part of the problem is, of course, that philosophers can easily de-vise different possibilities relating to the supposed existential journeys of souls—but how can one possibly judge between them? How can an incarnate, temporarily imprisoned soul, step outside itself in order to glimpse the greater scheme of things, and see where it fits into that scheme? The most obvious mechanism and method is that of dream-ing, and the idea is both very old and very powerful that it's possible, in principle, to obtain revelations of that kind in dreams. At the end of Plato's best-known dialogue, the *Republic*, Socrates tells the story of Er, who has a dream in which he foresees what will happen to his soul after death, witnesses souls selecting their future incarnations as various animals, and has a cosmic vision—of a geocentric cosmos, naturally—in which he perceives the harmony of the celestial spheres. The vision is al-legorical, of course, and different readers of Plato decode the allegory in different ways, but the fundamental idea is that if we could only persuade our dreams, somehow, to gift us with that greater consciousness, whether literal or allegorical, then we might be able to take a great leap forward in understanding the puzzle and purpose of our existence. In principle, we might be able to understand the how and why of the soul's existence prior to and subsequent to our present incarnation: the logic and mecha-nism of transanimation."

"And that's what Jim McKinnon and Christiane are trying to do?"

"It's been Jim's lifelong dream, at least since the late eighties. That's when he became convinced that psychotropic substances were the key to the revelation—but his induced dreams tended to disappear, just like his real ones, when he reverted to his normal waking state of mind. Arm-ing himself with a Dictaphone in order to record a verbal report of his experience only helped a little, because in his altered states of conscious-ness, he was unconcerned with making any such record—so he needed an observer, someone to engage him in conversation while he was in his altered state. I doubt that I'm the only one he's ever used, although I was surely the first…and perhaps because of that, he keeps coming back to me, at intervals, when he thinks he's found a new key to the problem.

He says it's because he trusts me, but really it's because he wants to convince me. The accidents of our personal history have appointed me as his examiner…or the person he thinks he has to defeat, in order to win his game.

"I'm also the person who has to stop him stabbing himself in the face. The first time, that idea really did come to him at random, and he was genuinely sorry that I got hurt wrestling with him. The second time…well, I don't know how deliberate it was, or how much of the deliberation was down to Jimmy and how much to his temporary craziness, but it definitely wasn't random. Next time…I mean this time, which was the next, from the viewpoint of the last, he hasn't taken the drug himself, yet. He's taken over my role, with respect to poor Christiane, and he seems to have convinced himself that he's done it well enough to come back to me, and that this time, he can pass the exam…or check-mate my incredulity"

"But he can't?"

"Of course not, because the whole edifice of ideas is nonsense, from beginning to end. There is no cosmic engineer, no immortal soul, no metempsychosis, no transanimation, no ultimate reason or ultimate good, no problem to be solved. That entire way of thinking, and everything about it, is just…wrong."

"Or yours is," she pointed out, unkindly.

"But it isn't," I was content to counter. It was late. I was tired; the cocoa was hot, thanks to Claire's microwave expertise, but I was drinking it as fast as I could, wishing that it were a better soporific than it really is.

She didn't question my certainty a second time; she knew how long that debate might take.

"I don't see any reason why I shouldn't take an interest," she said. "Maybe I can help you apply the brake, as you and he both seem to put it, if braking is really necessary. But the fact is, to be honest, that I'm already interested—curious, even. Just as you are…or we wouldn't be here, would we?"

I licked my lips, not simply to get rid of a little residual froth. I thought about Achilles' legendary heel…and about moths and flames. She was right, obviously. I was curious, I always had been. I'd always been too much of a coward ever to want to get a glimpse of what might lie beyond the cozy interior of my own carefully-wallpapered consciousness, but that didn't mean that I was immune to the fascination of the fantasy, or unwilling to let somebody else take the risks on my behalf… as long as it wasn't the foul-mouthed Mark Two, the mysterious stranger.

The trouble with looking outside, is that you really don't know what you might see. You might be searching for Eden or the Garden of the Hesperides, but there's always the danger of meeting the serpent or the dragon.

When I didn't say anything more, Claire stood up, and took her empty mug to the sink, where she filled it with water before leaving it on the side, so that the cocoa residue wouldn't set hard.

"I think Christiane might feel more comfortable, if she has to perform in front of an audience at all," she said, firmly, "if I were there as well as you. That's the impression I got. And in any case, I want to hear what her past selves have to say. Everyone needs a break from dull routine don't they?"

She was being sarcastic. She knew that I didn't…except that, when Jimmy McKinnon had turned up that afternoon, my reflex response, irrational as it might be, had been gladness rather than horror.

One way or another, though, I was beaten. It was her decision, and she seemed to have made it. All I could try to do was apply the brake gently, and try stop it going too far.

"Fine," I said. "Jimmy's always been a sucker for a good-looking woman. Perhaps you can make him see sense even though I never could."

"Thanks for the flattery," she said, on her way to the bathroom. "It's good to know that you're still prepared to take the trouble."

It would have been good to know that she was too, if in fact she was—but she didn't bail me out of that uncertainty.

VIII

The next day, when I came out of the school gates at five o'clock, Christiane Sacy was waiting for me, standing a few discreet yards behind the spot were Jimmy had been standing the day before. She had to take a couple of steps forward to meet me, whereas he had merely had to wait for the consequence of my momentum, like a mountain for Mahomet.

Naturally, my first impulse was to look around.

"Jim's off with some expediter from his company," she told me, "looking at flats and cottages that the company might commandeer on his behalf. He didn't want to take me with him, because I'm one of the things his employers don't need to know about, in his view. I've been kicking my heels all day, and watching the swans on the Thames really isn't much of a distraction. I thought of going to your house, but I wasn't sure I'd find anyone in, and I got the idea last night that you might not like that idea, so I thought I might buy you a cup of coffee instead. I'd really like to ask you a couple of questions, if you don't mind—in confidence."

"Oh," I said, caught at a loss. "Of course…"

There was no "of course" about it, really, given that it was definitely going behind Jimmy's back, even though I could imagine the smile he'd put on if he ever found out about it.

As before, there were still pupils filtering out in dribs and drabs after various after-school activities. If they'd been surprised to see the Head of History intercepted on a Monday by someone who looked like a down-market Indiana Jones, God alone know what they would think about seeing him accosted the day after by a woman with short-cropped hair and a tropical suntan, wearing what looked suspiciously like army fatigues. At any rate, I didn't hang around to attract further attention; we headed for Mount Pleasant.

It didn't take a genius to figure out what she wanted to know, and why she wanted to ask me "in confidence." She wanted to know about my previous collaborations with Jimmy's attempts to pry open the doors of perception. Doubtless Jimmy had told her about them all, but she presumably wanted a second opinion, from a different point of view.

When I asked her what I could get her, she asked for a double espresso. I doubted that she was afraid of getting a foam moustache on her upper lip, so I assumed that she felt the need for the intense caffeine boost.

It only took me a few minutes to summarize my three encounters with Jimmy's altered states of consciousness. I was deliberately brief, especially about the LSD episode and the biofeedback fiasco. It seemed, in any case, to be the third experiment in which she was most interested.

"I think I've met him," she said, casually, after I'd given her a verbal sketch of Mark Two.

"What do you mean?" I asked, more than a trifle nervously.

"When they carried Jim into the hospital, he was in a bad way. If we'd had ice, we would have packed him in it to bring his temperature down, but we didn't, so all we could do was keep him fully hydrated. We did what we could to bring him through the fever—what they used to call a *crisis* in the old days—but it really was touch and go for a few hours."

"And he was delirious? He talked?"

"Oh yes. Incoherently, of course, and incomprehensibly too…but there were snatches of near-clarity. It's not uncommon for patients to lose their inhibitions somewhat when delirious, to swear a lot and to seem aggressive…mercifully, he didn't actually become violent, or we'd have had to tie him down. It's also not unusual for them to lose track of time, to dredge things up from memory, for the years to…."

"Melt away?" I suggested.

"Something like that. Anyway, somebody had to sit with him, and it happened to be me. He mentioned Mark Two several times. It was gibberish at the time, obviously, and I just disregarded most of it, but much later, when he told me that he's made contact with some kind of alien intelligence that had called itself Mark Two while he was under the influenced of an entheogen…. I began to wish I'd listened a little more attentively, and tried a little harder to find the germ of sense within the confusion. And then, yesterday, I met you…Mark One, and began to wonder…."

She stopped. I prompted: "Wonder what?"

She took a moment, perhaps more for dramatic effect than to gather her thoughts. Then she said: "I presume you're wondering about me too—how crazy I might be. Well, who can tell? We all seem pretty sane to ourselves, don't we, even if we have our doubts? But I'm sane enough to hang on to my doubts. I've been interested in entheogens for a long time—you can't function in my line of work unless you're interested in the ideas and world-views of the people you're dealing with, and from their viewpoint, of course, there's little or no distinction between medical and religious practices. I'd taken entheogens, for the sake of curiosity, long before I met Jim, and undertaken my own philosophical explorations of the experiences I'd had. I've always tried to keep an open mind, as to whether I was really catching glimpses of what Jim calls hyperreality, or simply reprocessing the fugitive elements of my own subconscious. You'd probably classify me as credulous, but I hope you don't have me filed as a gullible fool."

I tried to assure her that I didn't, more by way of gestures than articulate statement. She was taking it for granted anyway, so she paid little or no heed to my efforts.

"Anyway," she went on," I try to keep the same balance in weighing Jim up. He's convinced that Mark Two really was an alien intelligence, of some kind…I don't mean extraterrestrial, but something displaced in time, an independent mental entity that managed to manifest itself in his brain under the influence of the entheogen. But…well, it must be even more obvious to you than it is to me that it's more probably some sort of construct of his subconscious mind, that it really is Mark Two: a distorted version of his image of you."

"If it was," I said, coldly, "then distorted is definitely the right word."

"Undoubtedly. Please don't take this the wrong way, but are you convinced that Jim really is as relentlessly and absolutely heterosexual as he pretends to be?"

I did take it the wrong way, but I tried not to let it show. "Speaking as his former wing-man," I said, "there's not an atom of doubt about it. Sometimes, if something walks like a duck, quacks like a duck and fucks like a duck, it really is a duck."

She didn't react to the obscenity—not at least in a prudish way. "Speaking as the duck he's currently fucking," she retorted, "I'm pretty much convinced myself…and I'm perfectly willing to believe that his attitude to you, and his conviction that he somehow needs your endorsement before he can allow himself to believe that he really has made intimate contact with hyperreality, is purely a matter of intellectual respect, or maybe the sense that you're some kind of counterpart to him, a polar opposite making up a thesis and antithesis, from which he needs to draw a synthesis. But the question remains: Are you, Mark One, the source of Mark Two? Are you the initial model on which his mind has built his twisted *alter ego*?"

"I don't know," I said, flatly, and was swift to counterpunch. "If I were, what would that make Sosipatra of Ephesus?"

She actually smiled. "Touché," she said. "I've been wondering that myself."

"Did you have a model in mind?" I queried.

"If that's a subtle way of throwing my own question back at me and asking me whether I'm as un-straight as I look, I like to think of myself as versatile—but no, I can't think of anyone I know, or have known, who might have served as a model for Sosipatra. I suppose you wouldn't believe me if I told you that I'd never heard of her, or had any inkling that any such person had ever existed, until I started checking the tapes that Jimmy made against Wikipedia?"

"Oh, I believe that you had no conscious recollection of ever having heard of her," I assured her.

"That's weaseling, and you know it. By means of that strategy, you could attribute absolutely anything I or anyone else discovered in an altered state of consciousness to an unconscious memory."

"Indeed," I agreed. "So can you, it seems, at least with respect to Mark Two."

She nodded. "I can see why Jim insisted that we come to you before coming to a final judgment on what we've accomplished," she said. "Unnecessary, in my opinion—I can do that myself, even if Jim can't. But it is frustrating, listening to your supposed alter ego on tape *and not being able to remember*. If that God's little joke, he's got a wicked sense of humor."

"It's not a joke," I told her. "It's a necessary protective measure. And it's not God's, it's our own. It's the heroic action of our own sanity, our own reason, our own sense of the good. Because we know, at least when we're awake and rational, that it really isn't good for us to lose our grip on the reality of things, and the necessity of things. That way lies madness."

"You're probably right," she said, with a sigh. "But also temptation. Once you've caught the glimpse…do you seriously imagine that now I've heard myself on tape channeling Sosipatra, I could simply forget her? Could you forget something similar?"

"It would be difficult," I admitted, although the thought that actually occurred to me was that there was no way on earth that anything similar was ever going to rear its ugly head from the abyssal depths of my mind.

She obviously guessed that.

"And that's why you're so adamant that you're never going to take the risk, isn't it?" she said. "That's why you looked as if the Devil had just materialized in your dining-room last night when Claire said she wanted to try Jim's entheogen?"

"Did I?" I asked, anxiously.

"Yes," she confirmed. "But don't take offense—I'm truly sorry if I'm coming across as a trifle aggressive. Please make allowances for the fact that I'm way out of my element here. I really would like us to be on the same side, because I think Jim is closer to the truth than he realizes when he says that your judgment might be invaluable to this exploration. Obviously, you and I can't be friends in the sense that you and he are, but…I don't have anybody else. Can you understand what I mean by that?"

To be honest, I felt profoundly glad that she'd come to me instead of going to Claire, although it was perfectly logical that she would. I was the person in the know, the expert…except that I wasn't really. I hadn't seen Jimmy for ten years; I had no idea where he was up to in his own thinking. Not that he would necessarily have worked out his own philosophical position in any kind of coherent fashion, given that he was a practical man.

Christiane, on the other hand, did seem to be something of a theoretician, a person with whom it was possible to debate an issue rationally.

"In your heart of hearts," I asked her, "do you really believe in metempsychosis?"

"In my mind of minds," she countered, "I wish I knew. But Sosipatra believes it, if the tapes can be trusted. It's frustrating, of course, to know her indirectly, through reports made in my own voice, but not to be aware of her, or even to remember her. She has a big advantage over me there, because she knows all about me…which is humiliating, as well as worrying."

"Why?" I asked.

"Because, if the tapes can be trusted, she doesn't think much of me. You'll see that, I guess, when you meet her…at which point, you'll have an advantage over me too, because I never have. I can only listen to her voice on tape, but you'll be able to look into her eyes, and feel her looking into yours. You'll probably be safe, though. You're not in any danger of falling in love with her, and she doesn't have anything against you."

I had to decide which of the various elements of that peculiar statement to query; I decided on the second. "You think Sosipatra has something against you?" I repeated.

"Well…as I said, she doesn't seem to think much of me. I suppose she has grounds, with her being a miracle-worker and a seeress, and me just being a glorified nurse, but even so…to hear the contempt in her voice—my voice—when she refers to me. It's not nice."

"And have you examined yourself carefully for possible reasons for subconscious self-dissatisfaction?" I asked her, trying to frame it so that it didn't sound too unkind.

"Of course I have," she said, "and sometimes I'm distressed to discover how easy it is to find them—but she's convinced me, as well as Jim, that she really is a different person, and not just a sly way for my superego to scourge me with criticism. And you were wrong, by the way, when you told Jim that she was just another carbon-copy miracle-worker invented as a feeble counter-measure to Christian propaganda. Whether she was a genuine prophetess or not, there's definitely more to her than that. Even if she's only a mental construct devised by my subconscious, there's much more to her than that."

"In what way?" I asked, genuinely interested.

"For one thing, because she has an inkling of the true complexity of the situation, and the true nature of time, that Plato and Proclus, for all their genius, didn't have. It's not just that they imagined a limited, geocentric universe, with a similarly restricted notion of celestial souls, imagining the plenitude of being in the narrow context of the beings with which they were familiar. They also imagined that plenitude as being a fundamentally steady state, whose evolution was linear in a temporal sense. You understand all that, right? You've done the reading. Jim says that you would have."

"I understand. So why was Sosipatra different, in your estimation?"

"Firstly, because she envisages time as a closed loop, with no beginning or end, so that past and future ultimately fused—not as a simple circle, but as an exceedingly complex knot."

"The tangled web of time," I observed. "It's always been one of Jimmy's catch-phrases. So what?"

"So, Sosipatra has a sense of the real extent of space and time; she doesn't think of space as a simple set of crystal spheres around the earth, or time as simply calendrical time magnified a few thousand or million times. I don't say that when she was alive she had a sense of space as modern astronomy envisages it, or the billons and trillions of years of time over which astronomers now envisage the age of the universe of galaxies, but she knows that the universe is truly vast, and she knows that that the notion of the human soul that Pythagoras, Plato and Proclus had was far too limited."

"What Jim calls the rubber ball theory of the soul, bouncing from body to body?" I supplied, helpfully.

"If you like," she conceded. "What we need, you see, in order to adapt a theory of metempsychosis to the image of the universe developed with the aid of modern astronomy and biology, is a notion of the soul that isn't something tiny and traveling, but something vast and everlasting, something that undergoes local metamorphoses—local in both space and time—but which never separates itself entirely, never encloses itself entirely, which has always existed and always will, because it has no beginning and no end."

I didn't know enough science to know whether the paradoxical wonderland of modern theoretical physics could accommodate a sealed loop of time, and I didn't suppose for a moment that she did either, but I didn't think that it particularly relevant to the core of the argument.

"The problem with that," I said, "is that if you want to save anything substantial of the classical theory, then you have to adapt the supposed moral order of the universe to it. Where and how does *the good* fit into it? Where in the tangled web of time does perfection lie, for the infinitely elastic soul?"

"I don't know," she said. "That's what Jim and I are trying to figure out, with Sosipatra's help."

"You can, I suppose, argue from the principle of plenitude: that just as the spatial universe needs to contain everything it can contain, in order to be whole, wholeness being construed as a necessary aspect of goodness, so the soul, distributed through the tangled knot of time, needs to experience every possible moral state, symbolized by every possible incarnation...that in order for the soul to be properly whole and thus properly good, it has to have experience of the possibilities of evil. That way, moral evolution wouldn't need to be a matter of climbing a ladder and sometimes slipping back down again after a false step. It would be a matter of the soul learning to know the truth of itself, and to focus that self-knowledge in the state of perfection, compared and contrasted with its mature and regretful awareness of all the stress of imperfection that it's necessary to experience in order to appreciate perfection."

I was rather pleased with that analysis—without, of course, believing a single word of it.

"I suppose you could," said Christiane.

I took the logical inference: "But you don't?"

"That doesn't seem to be the way that my...acquaintance with Sosipatra is going."

"Where is it going, then?"

"If I knew that, we'd already be there. If she knows, she hasn't put it on tape yet. But Jim thinks we're getting there. Maybe she'll explain it to you, when you meet her. Jim certainly wants her to do it...in fact, he's explicitly challenged her to do it, as a kind of test...not just of her powers, but of her reality."

I had to remind myself that she was really talking about herself, that it was really to her that the challenge had been issued—and that it was really her, not Sosipatra, who wanted to please Jimmy, to make him a present of the grail of which he was in quest.

"Jimmy always thinks he's getting there," I told her. "But he never does and never will. You shouldn't take that personally, Christiane. It's his failure, not yours."

"But if he succeeds," she countered. "It will be my success too. I've never got there any more than he has...but we never had Sosipatra before...or one another."

"And how, exactly, do you see that working out?" I asked, trying to sound sympathetic. "I presume that you're not thinking of getting married, settling down somewhere and producing a little Melody of your own...but even within the context of the quest for enlightenment, how do you see it working out? What happens after Sosipatra gives you the key to the secret of the universe, the true nature of the soul's existence in the tangled web of time, and the true purpose of the universe, and your own life, if she can and if she's willing? What will you do with it?"

"I don't know," she said, a trifle wistfully, "but I know I'd rather have it than not have it, if it's accessible. I know that I'd feel better for having it."

And that, of course, was the kernel within the nutshell. The point wasn't so much what she might get out of it, because she wasn't the kind of foolish optimist who might think that it was going to provide her with eternal youth or fabulous wealth, or even a happy marriage. The point was that she wasn't happy where and when she was, with what she was. She was in search of a better state of mind: an alternative state of consciousness in which she could live more contentedly than the one she had. And I couldn't point her in the right direction, even though I'd found such a state of being myself, because I knew full well that what I'd found was only what I had always wanted, and that it didn't and couldn't work for everyone. All I'd ever been able to do for Jimmy was try to stop him from going too far off the rails; there had never been any possibility of his pulling into my particular station. He wasn't me. In fact, he was my opposite, my antithesis, and there was no way I could even imagine him ever reaching the grail he sought.

By some uncanny coincidence, both our phones stated buzzing at the same moment. Jimmy was calling Christiane and Claire was calling me, to update us on where they were up to in the hectic routine of their day.

Neither of us reciprocated by specifying where we were, or with whom. Our own conversation was confidential.

"Jimmy thinks he's found us somewhere to stay," Christiane reported, afterwards. "Do you know a place called Church Crookham?"

"I know where it is," I confirmed. "It's east of Basingstoke—only a village twenty years ago, but massively expanded with housing developments since then, and fused with the neighboring town of Fleet. Supposed to be very pleasant, though—Fleet won some kind of poll conducted by a building society to identify the place with the best quality of life in the UK. I don't believe it, myself."

"You do surprise me," she said, sarcastically.

"Claire's still at work," I supplied, in my turn, "but she hopes to be home shortly. She wants me to cook."

"Well, I suppose I shouldn't hold you up, then," she said, getting up and preparing to leave. "I'd better get back to the hotel anyway, to meet Jim. But thanks for answering my questions—and it's been interesting. I hope I haven't bored you."

"Of course not," I assured her, sincerely.

"And I feel slightly better now about the prospect of your seeing me…naked, as it were, with my mental clothing stripped away."

I looked her in her softly sparkling eyes. "You do realize, don't you," I said, that what you're doing is mortally dangerous?"

"Of course," she replied, simply.

"But?" I prompted.

She looked embarrassed. "But he's worth it," he said. Not *it*, or *she*, but *he*.

I nodded. "I'll do what I can to help," I told her, knowing that it was a hollow assurance.

She took a step toward the door, but hesitated. "I do have a favor to ask, though…."

"What's that?"

"Bring Claire. I know you don't want to, but…I'd rather you did. Is that okay?"

"Of course," I said. I figured that it wouldn't do any harm for her to think that I was doing her a favor, even though I knew perfectly well that I couldn't have kept Claire out of it now, even if I'd wanted to.

"It won't get out of hand," she assured me. "I'll see to that."

She was promising far too much; because I knew that she had no more control or authority than I did, but all I said was: "Thanks."

She didn't offer her cheek for a mock-kiss, or her hand to be shaken; she barely contrived a farewell nod. And so we parted, going in opposite directions, for the moment—but both, presumably, with the same ultimate destination in mind.

IX

When I got home, Melody was in the sitting room, apparently doing nothing. She didn't even have the TV on. When I went in she looked up from her armchair and said, in a mock-accusatory tone: "You're late."

Reflexively, I said: "I got held up at school"—an excuse so worn out that it slid off the tongue without the slightest effort.

"No you didn't" she said, in a tone that I couldn't accurately evaluate, but had a hint of smugness in it. "You were in the coffee-shop on Mount Pleasant with Christiane Sacy."

I felt a kind of electric shock. I don't know what color I turned.

"Don't worry," she said. "I haven't been following you. I got a tip."

"A tip?" I queried.

"We don't live in a bubble, Dad—at least, I don't. My school is only a few hundred yards from yours, and yours being all boys and mine being all girls, we socialize, especially in the sixth-form. I know a lot of the boys in the parallel year. So, if you don't want news of your secret assignations getting back to me, don't arrange them for the school gate. You'd probably hardly said hello before a little bird called to say that you'd been seen heading west with, as he put it, a 'lezzer with a shell-suit and an overdone fake tan.' It didn't take a genius to work out who he meant."

My memory automatically went back to the school gate, seeking to identify the bird in question and put him down on my grudge list, but I hadn't been paying enough attention to the uniformed oiks sidling past during the interval in question.

"I suppose it was a shell-suit of sorts," I managed to say, "but I still have to give him an F for observation." Then I was quick to add: "She wanted to ask me a couple of questions, in confidence."

"That's all right," she said. "I won't shop you to Mum. Questions about your friend Jim?"

"Yes," I said.

"She really ought to have waited her turn. I have a few of those myself."

"Really? Why?"

"Oh, come on Dad. I see him once, when I'm about eight or so, and he's nice to me, in the patronizing sort of way that adults are nice to eight-year-olds, and gives me the impression that he's one of your dearest friends, and then I don't hear a single mention of him again, ever, until he suddenly turns up for dinner, back from New Guinea with a nurse he met in a field hospital, who spends the evening talking about all your drug-assisted experiments in past life regression, and you don't think I have a right to be curious?"

"Mum wants me to make dinner," I said. "She'll be home shortly. I'd better get started."

Naturally, she followed me into the kitchen, and didn't volunteer to peel the potatoes. I decided that I'd bake them, instead of peeling them myself, so I stuck them in the microwave for five minutes so that I could finish them off in the oven thereafter, along with the steak pie that Claire had thoughtfully removed from the freezer that morning.

"Honestly, Dad," she said, "I didn't know you had it in you. You and LSD? I'm mean, I've tried *es* and pot, and a few legal highs, but...." She broke off.

I think I could actually feel the blood draining out of my face.

"Oh, right," she said. "Mum never told you. That's good, I guess. You didn't think I was a virgin as well, did you?"

"Actually," I said, very faintly, "Yes." I was still vaguely hoping that she was going to say: "Joke!"

She didn't.

"Right," she said, again. "Well, I guess the *don't ask don't tell* rule just went out the window. For what's worth, though, I thought it was all overrated—cannabis, ecstasy, even sex, although that might have had more to do with particular circumstances. With the drugs, I guess you have to be in the right frame of mind. You brought me up too well—I always went into it skeptically, and came out the same way. But you...."

"I never took LSD," I hastened to add. "Jimmy did, but I just looked after him when he was tripping, to make sure that he didn't do anything stupid. He got hooked, in an odd sort of way, and he came back to me a couple of times, so I could do the same again. I never took anything."

"Oh," she said. "And you never had sex until your wedding night with Mum?"

"Oh, come on, Mel!" I complained.

"All right," she said. "Didn't mean to embarrass you. I'm eighteen, you know—I'll be leaving home soon. I need to know what kind of world I'm going into, don't I? And to set your mind at rest, you were right—about everything."

"What?"

"You were right—you and Mum. Probably best to leave mind-bending drugs alone, and not risk your clarity of mind for no great reward, and probably best to stick to sex with people with whom you might actually want to form a lasting relationship. But you can't blame me for checking, can you?"

Couldn't I? It seemed a little like lack of trust to me. On balance, though, dipping her toes in the water didn't seem to have done her much harm—provided that she wasn't pregnant. I daren't ask, but I made a metal note to ask Claire to make sure.

"You've taken ecstasy?" I queried.

"I think so, Rumor has it that a lot of the stuff that gets sold as ecstasy these days is a mixture of speed and LSD, but I think it was the real thing—not that it lived up to its name. If only your mate Jim had turned up this time last year, a connection like that could have made me really popular at school. A guy who actually invents new highs for a living! All that and past lives too! Too late now, though…my schooldays are over, bar the shouting."

"Jimmy," I told her, "would not deal drugs to schoolchildren—or anyone else for that matter."

"Except for nurses from Third World field hospitals who fix up sneaky dates with my Dad behind my Mum's back—and Jim's too, I suppose?"

"Damn it, Mel, it's not like that. None of it. Jimmy's just had this bee in his bonnet for thirty years, and he's managed to find someone with a similar interest. He's not a drug dealer and she's not a user, and she certainly isn't trying to seduce me behind your mother's back. She wanted to know more about the experiments Jimmy had done in the past, to which I was the only witness. It's perfectly understandable, and entirely reasonable that she wanted to do it discreetly—not realizing, being entirely out of her native cultural environment, that intercepting me at the school gate the way Jimmy had the day before would set the jungle drums beating all the way back to you."

"But you are going to help them with their so-called experiments, aren't you? You and Mum?"

"Jimmy wants me to," I said, defensively.

"And Christiane? Does she want you to?"

I stuck to a bare "Yes." It seemed sufficient, at least to me.

"But not me. Nobody wants me—least of all you."

"Everybody wants you to be safe," I said. "Most of all your Mum and me."

"Is what you're doing illegal?" she demanded.

"No."

"Then what's unsafe about it?"

"It's not a sideshow, Mel."

"No, it's an experiment. An educational experiment. Something I might only have the chance to see once in a lifetime. Unless, of course…."

She stopped again, deliberately teasing me with the possibility that her experimental phase might not be over yet.

She was eighteen. She was an adult, not merely technically but in her own estimation. And she was stubborn. She hadn't only got that from her mother. I couldn't just issue an edict. I had to find another way.

I transferred the microwaved potatoes to the oven with the pie, tipped frozen peas into a pan, covered them with water and switched on the hotplate. Then I checked my watch, half-wishing that Claire was already home, and half-wondering what she might say if she walked in on the conversation and wanted to be brought up to date with what she'd missed.

"It's Jimmy's experiment," I said. "He wants me there, for form's sake. He'll allow Claire in, under protest—but he won't go any further than that."

"I could talk him into it," she said. "Or Christiane, come to that."

"Mel!" There was more agony than scandal in my tone.

"But I won't," she hastened to add. "I'll be good. But you can't blame me for being interested, can you? You can't blame me for wanting to know how it goes—and you won't blame me for asking, will you, if I can't actually join the committee. I mean, the *don't ask don't tell* rule went out of the window last night, didn't it, when Christiane opened her big mouth and blew it?"

She was right; Claire and I had bought her up far too well; we'd taught her to be intelligent, independent and skeptical. And she was— leaving us blown sky high by our own petard.

"Actually," I told her, "I'm not at all sure that I'm going to go ahead with it. It's already got out of hand. I should never have brought Jimmy home last night—or ten years ago, come to that. I should have learned my lesson at nineteen, but you know how kids are, don't you? Maybe it's time to stop and wash my hands of it. While it was just between the two of us, it was one thing, but now…I really don't think I ought to be party to it any more."

At least she wasn't bold enough just to tell me that I was talking bullshit. "Are you serious?" she asked.

"Perfectly," I said.

"You'd really let an opportunity like this pass you by?"

"An opportunity like what?"

"Hell, Dad, you know perfectly well. What if he's right? What if he really has enabled Christiane to access a past life? What if he can enable everyone to do it? Do you really not want to be there when the world might be about to change?"

"It isn't," I told her.

She wasn't bold enough to tell me that I might be mistaken, either.

"And Mum?" she said, instead.

And that was checkmate. I could, in theory, drop out myself—but what would I say to Claire, especially now I'd practically promised Christiane, and well as her, to bring her in. I knew that there was no way back, now. It was too late. It had got out of hand.

Because I didn't say anything, Melody didn't know that I'd admitted defeat. "If you're not there," she said, "he'll take the drug himself, won't he?"

"He's going to take it anyway, sooner or later," I said. "Wild horses wouldn't stop him. It doesn't matter what Christiane's make-believe Sosipatra of Ephesus does or doesn't say under the influence. Sooner or later, he'll stop fluttering around the candle and burn himself…unless I can find a way to demonstrate to him that that he shouldn't."

"And how can you do that?"

It was a good question. But in the past, I had, not once but, apparently, twice. Both times, it had been the shock and alarm of having hurt someone else—me—that had given him pause, made him abandon LSD and ayahusaca and move on. Could I do it again, preferably without getting stabbed in the eye? But that wasn't a direction in which I wanted to direct my train of thought. I was about to switch the points, deliberately, but I'd paused for too long, and Melody had moved on.

"Is that's why he wants you there, do you think?" she asked. "Because, subconsciously, he wants you to stop him?"

It was an interesting hypothesis, but I couldn't believe it.

"You don't know Jimmy," I told her. "He just wants to show off, to demonstrate his cleverness, his success, his triumph." But then, uncharacteristically, I began to doubt myself. "At least, that's what he tells himself," I muttered. I didn't add anything further.

"What do you mean?"

I didn't know, exactly. I was confused. Things were happening too quickly; everything was becoming tangled. But everything around me was in order, proceeding according to plan. The peas were simmering quietly; the pie was in the oven; there was nothing else to do but let everything idle for ten minutes, and then keep it all warm if Claire still wasn't home.

"I think what he really wants to do, whether he knows it consciously or not," I improvised, grasping the nearest available straw "is to prove something to me. He wants to prove that, for thirty years, he's been in the right and I've been in the wrong. We're counterparts, you see: yin and yang. One of us has to be wrong, if the other is right."

"Ah!" said my darling daughter, whom Claire and I'd brought up far too well. "And you need to prove to him that you're right, and he's wrong, just as much as he needs the opposite." She didn't add a rider about whether I was consciously aware of it or not. She didn't need to. It was an opportunity for me to admire her intelligence, perhaps even to congratulate myself for having nurtured it so successfully—but all I was feeling was *ouch!*

And then the front door banged, and Claire came in.

She came straight to the kitchen, and said: "Just in time," by the look of things—but the table's not laid." She looked at Melody, accusingly.

"It's my fault," I hastened to say. "We were chatting." Bad move.

"About what?"

"Just this and that," Melody said, swiftly. Her eyes were fixed on me, and I realized that I wasn't the only one who didn't want too much said. She didn't want me to mention her drug record and lack of virginity, even though Claire already knew about them. She wanted her mother to think that that was still just between the two of them.

"It's all right," Claire said blithely. "I know exactly what you were talking about."

"Really?" said Melody, with admirable skepticism.

"Of course. After a dinner party like last night's what other topic of conversation could there be? And your dear father has doubtless been spouting off at tedious length about why it's absolutely impossible for souls to be reincarnated and for people to recover ancestral memories. I'm right, aren't I?"

"Absolutely," I said.

"And very convincing he is, too," said my adorable daughter, supportively. "Not that he wasn't preaching to the choir, mind. Although it might have been nice to find out that I'd been Cleopatra in a previous life, or Catherine the Great. Oh, sorry…I mean Florence Nightingale, obviously, or Elizabeth Fry."

"Obviously," Claire agreed, skepticallly. To me, she said: "Have you heard from Jim?"

"No," I said—it was true, after all. "But we will. You can depend on it." Then I hurried out to lay the table, Melody having made no move in that direction. For once, I didn't hold it against her.

X

Jimmy being Jimmy, he didn't ring until nine o'clock Friday night to tell us that he and Christiane were comfortably ensconced in a nice furnished cottage in Church Crookham, that they'd unpacked their trunks, that it was "all go for tomorrow," and that he's pick us up bright and early in the car. There was no point in telling him that it was ludicrously short notice, and reminding him no formal arrangement had ever been made. Claire had cleared her schedule in anticipation; we were all set.

I can't say that I was entirely happy about the fact that we were leaving Melody behind, now that I had some inkling of what she got up to when we weren't around, but I would have been even less happy about taking her with us. When I kissed her forehead to say goodbye she put on an exaggerated show of demure reserve and promised me that she wouldn't do anything I wouldn't do—which was only partly reassuring, especially as she offered her cheek to "Uncle Jim" for him to kiss too, while looking at me as if to remind me that if she only took the trouble to flutter her eyelashes, she was fully convinced that she could lever an invitation to come with us out of our prospective host.

Christiane hadn't come with Jim to pick us up; apparently she was doing the shopping and preparing the guest-room. I took the front passenger seat and Claire got in the back.

"It's a bit close to Basingstoke for my liking," Jim said, speaking of Church Crookham, once we were under way and heading south. "As the Company are paying the rent on the cottage, they'll probably regard me as being on call. I suspect they have a rather flexible idea of the meaning of the phrase 'medical leave,' even with the word compulsory stuck in front of it."

"But at least you get the chance to use their labs," I pointed out, trying to be helpful, although why I should have wanted to put in a good word for Basingstoke I had no idea.

"Ha!" he said. "If you only knew. Sure, I can get lab time, if I fill in all the forms. Sure, I can requisition any substance under the sun, as long as I fill in all the fucking forms. In Pom Town, you know, I'm the big wheel. Everyone in Moresby knows that if it weren't for my endeavors and those of a handful of other guys following religiously in my footsteps, the establishment wouldn't even exist. When I say jump, all any-one ever says in reply is 'how high?' And even in Darwin, I get respect. I'm McKinnon the fixer, McKinnon the man who knows what's what and gets things done, McKinnon the guy that the UN programs and MSF rely on to help them out when they're in a jam. But not in Basingstoke. I mean, it's not as if the guys at the top don't know exactly what I do and exactly what it's worth, but the problem is the local pen-pushers and penny-counters. Here, I'm just the hick from the outback who's a bloody nuisance because he wants a cottage to live in while he serves out his term of penitentiary leave."

"So you haven't spent the last week brewing customized entheo-gens?"

"Chance would be a fine thing. I'm a bit short, as it goes, with hav-ing been at death's door and all, but I still have the fag end of the last Moresby batch, so I'm okay for a couple of weeks. After that—well, I'll just have to sweet-talk a couple of the girls into looking the other way for an hour or two. Don't worry, everything will be okay."

"As long as MSF don't summon Christiane abruptly to the Ivory Coast or Costa Rica to help out with some epidemic," I said.

"Don't joke about such things," he said. "They can happen."

"Presumably it will, sooner or later," Claire put in. "Will one or other of you be able to negotiate your postings so that you end up in the same place?"

"It's theoretically possible," was all that Jimmy would admit.

"But that's not the kind of world you live in, is it?" I said. "It's a soci-ety of disposable relationships, where everyone hooks up with whoever happens to be around at the time, for as long as the posting lasts…or not even as long as that."

"This is what the logic of the situation tends to dictate," Jimmy con-ceded.

"But it doesn't matter," I supplied, a trifle maliciously, "because you and Christiane aren't planning to be together for long anyway, are you? Just long enough to finish your experimental run. It's not as if you're in love, is it?"

"Christiane's great," he assured me. "Much better than either of my wives, with the aid of hindsight, but she's very committed to her job, and very good at it too. MSF will almost certainly call her back to Indonesia, though not necessarily to Jiwaka. My bosses might well send me back there too, given my local knowledge, but the ways of Big Pharma are essentially mysterious, so we'd be fools to bet on it. We don't need to be bunking together to carry on the work, though. Even in a godforsaken hole like Jiwaka you can get Skype. In a couple of years the locals will be setting up their own live porn feeds there, trying to take business from the Philippines."

"Let's hope we don't run out of pigs and hyenas for all those degraded human souls to be reborn into," I said. "The men, that is, not the poor girls."

"Mark always feels sorry for the poor girls," Claire put in, with a hint of *double entendre*.

"Oh, there's no shortage of cockroaches out there," Jim assured us, breezily. "Big ones, too. If Proclus was right about human evil being necessary in order to supply the viler creatures of the Earth with suitable transanimated individuality, supplying the vermin of the Far East must require a hell of a lot of human vice. There simply aren't enough Americans to go around, and they live far too long."

"If my superficial reading can be trusted," I said, "Proclus didn't include insects in his hierarchy of souls. That doesn't mean that we shouldn't, of course—but where do we stop? Do the residues of human evil have to supply souls to malarial parasites, bacteria and viruses."

"It doesn't work like that," Jimmy assured me. "You're still thinking of souls as neat discrete packages that bounce from one body to another as they die."

Actually I wasn't. I was just thinking that Proclus seemed to have been thinking along those lines. I didn't doubt, either, than anyone trying to extrapolate his thinking into the context of modern biology could easily have found a means of rigging the arithmetic. I'd already had enough of that kind of hypothesis-chopping. Doubtless we'd get back to it later, though, when Jimmy unveiled his new psychotropic miracle and Sosipatra came out of hiding in Christian's subconscious to play the game in something akin to earnest.

I realized that I really was looking forward to meeting Sosipatra, although, as Claire had cattily remarked, I couldn't help feeling sorry for poor Christiane.

I searched for a different topic of conversation, but I was still hesitating when Jimmy remarked: "Your daughter is very charming now she's grown up."

"If your next sentence begins 'If I were thirty years younger,' I'll strangle you," I said.

"God, no," said Jimmy. "I wouldn't wish a waste of space like my younger self on the poor kid. Anyway, she's your daughter—far too much common sense to go for someone like my nineteen-year-old self. She'll be looking for someone to settle down with and be happy—I won't say someone just like you, if you don't mind, but someone reliable, someone…decent."

"If you're shopping for compliments," I said, "you've come to the wrong boutique."

"I wasn't," Jimmy said, with enough bitterness in his tone to convince me that he meant it. "I certainly won't say that it's been a curse that I've always found it relatively easy to get women to fall in love with me, but it certainly hasn't been an unalloyed godsend. At nineteen, I thought I was God's gift—but I wasn't, was I?"

"It was hardly my opinion that mattered," I observed, "and speaking as your old wing-man, I have to admit that you had me convinced. But I'm willing to accept your mature judgment that you weren't."

"Very kind of you," I remarked. "Yours, I assume, is a back-handed compliment boutique?"

"The customer is always right," I quipped.

"Not in the pharma business," he quipped back. "There, the customer is always ill, whether he knows it or not." With only the briefest of pauses, he added: "I'm glad that Christiane's tough enough not to fall for it—the God's gift delusion, that is."

"Is she?" I asked, try not to challenge the assertion too blatantly.

"Oh yes. Old boots have nothing on her—toughness-wise, that is. She's a very attractive lady, as you've seen, although you haven't seen her naked. I can't any longer muster the kind of white heat of passion that came so easily when I was young, but believe me, I'm as fond of her as I can be of anyone nowadays."

"I'm sure she'd be delighted by the compliment," Claire put in, from the back seat.

"Oh, she knows the score," said Jimmy. "If you get to have a girly chat with her, I'm sure she'll talk about me in even more lukewarm terms. We can't all be as steadfast as you and Mark, especially those of us who don't live in your world—but Chris and I will do for one another, for the time being. Just because we won't be taking early retirement from field-work, getting married, buying a cottage in Church Crookham and growing roses in the garden, it doesn't mean that we aren't happy."

"Nobody said it did," I pointed out, which was a lot more diplomatic than saying: *But you aren't, are you?*—which was what I actually thought.

"I've always been glad for you, Mark," he said. "I don't say that I envy you, mind, but I've always been glad for you."

"Thanks," sdaid Claire, dryly.

"Oh, please don't put me on that spot," Jimmy complained. "I can't say that of course I envy him you without upsetting him, and I can't say I don't without insulting you, so let's just leave it at I'm glad that he has you, because you make him happy, as you would any sane man, shall we?"

"Of course," she said, graciously. "And I'm sure he's equally glad that you have Christiane, aren't you, darling?"

"Absolutely," I said, complaisantly, just as if she hadn't meant it sarcastically. But was I, though? How could I be glad, really, that he'd found someone to encourage his obsession, to enter into a *folie à deux* with him? On the other hand why shouldn't I, if Christiane really was as tough as old boots? But was she? In her abnormal state of consciousness, perhaps....

I let it go. It was too confused, and too confusing.

Because it was Saturday and still early, the Basingstoke Road wasn't as busy as it was on weekdays; we reached Fleet in good time, and Church Crookham, from there, in practically no time at all.

The cottage really was a cottage, not an item of recent pastiche just pretending. It had been thoroughly refitted internally, though, with what estate agents used to call "all mod cons" and a few extra ones besides, including an authentic drinks cabinet, albeit only stocked, for the moment, with a single bottle of blended whisky, from which a couple of fingers had already been drawn off. The guest bedroom was small but the bed was a good size, and the kitchen, at least, was still tidy.

We went out for a walk before lunch, in order to enjoy the summer air and the authentic English rural environment, but Jim's impatience was only superficially repressed, and Christiane didn't seem overly impressed. It probably seemed a trifle tame by comparison with the promenades around Jiwaka.

We ate lunch in the local pub, which was crowded. Even though Jimmy had no plans to get behind the wheel again, he limited himself to a single pint. Christiane had a pint of so-called real ale herself, more in a spirit of experimentation, I assumed, than to emphasize her slightly masculine appearance, although she obviously hadn't taken any steps as yet to acquire a feminine wardrobe. Why should she? She didn't have anything to prove, and she was among friends.

Afterwards, Jimmy took over.

It was showtime.

XI

There was no yellow-stained sugar-lump this time, but no gleaming hypodermic either. There was a wall-safe; seemingly, that was a standard among the extra mod cons that Jimmy's employers installed when adapting the properties they bought, so that their important guests could lock away their miscellaneous valuables. All that Jimmy had put in his, and all that he took out of it, with due reverence, was an ordinary plastic pill-box with one of those "child-proof" tops that people of my generation always find it so difficult to open. Jimmy was a professional, though; he popped the cap with a practiced twist-and-flick.

He showed me the contents: maybe two dozen nondescript white pills, with no identifying stamp and no sugar coat, as one would expect if they were vintage Port Moresby. The box didn't have a label, let alone a little skull and crossbones to serve as a warning if it should happen to fall, by some unforeseeable accident, into the wrong hands.

Judging purely by appearances, the pills could have been anything, including a placebo—but I was morally certain that they weren't a placebo.

Jimmy had bought a brand new digital voice recorder. I didn't recognize the model, but I knew that it was light years ahead of the antiquated tape-machine we had used back in the old days, and could undoubtedly record for more than twenty-four hours if need be. Jimmy didn't hook Christiane up to any kind of machine, or put on any show of sending her into some kind of hypnotic state himself. He just handed her a pill, along with a glass of water, and she sat down in an armchair.

Jimmy went back to the safe, scrupulously replaced the box of pills, shut the door, gave the combination-wheel a token spin, and came back to sit down in a second armchair, facing his protégée. Claire and I had sat down together on a sofa, placed laterally to one side of the facing armchairs.

After having swallowed the pill, Christiane put the glass, still half-full of water, on a small table beside her chair.

Then we waited.

Time dragged a little, partly because we sat in silence, simply waiting. Jimmy didn't seem at all anxious; he was confident. Christiane seemed a little drowsy, and she lay back in the armchair—but it was a warm afternoon, and we'd had a walk in the open air and a pub lunch. It would have been surprising if she hadn't been a trifle somnolent. If it hadn't been for the sense of expectation, I might have dozed off myself. Christiane seemed quite serene.

There was no dramatic change to begin with. The shift was subtle—but Christiane did change, and Sosipatra came out to play, as her subconscious switched into personality-synthesizing mode. At first, I thought it was simply her expression that changed, as the appearance of somnolence was dispelled and she became alert and attentive again, but I got the impression soon enough that her features really had altered. It wasn't that they became prettier, or even more feminine, and she didn't lose her tropical tan, but they shifted, and she became a different person.

Then there was a lag phase, during which her new features twitched, as if she were going through a rapid sequence of mood-shifts, in which all kinds of expressions, ranging from ecstasy to distress, overlapped momentarily. But she stiffened in her seat, apparently asserting control, pulling herself together. She blinked twice, and her face became serene again.

She looked round, curiously, but not as if she had no idea where she was. Her gaze didn't linger long on Jimmy, moving on swiftly, as if he were too familiar to require closer examination. It lingered a good deal longer in Claire, and then on me. There was a slight smile on Christiane's new face—Sosipatra's face, I assumed—but I couldn't tell which of us had occasioned it, or why.

Jimmy reached over and switched on the voice-recorder.

"Sosipatra?" he said.

"If you like, my love," Christiane replied—in her own voice, pronouncing the word "my love" just as she had the first time I'd seen her.

"I know that you're more than that," Jimmy said. "Much more. But you really are Sosipatra of Ephesus, aren't you? Or once were, from our time-limited viewpoint."

"Yes, my love."

"And you really were a seeress, able to see into what we would call the future?"

"Yes."

"And you had abilities that convinced people who knew you that you were a miracle-worker?"

"Yes."

So far, I thought, so unimpressive. If all that she was going to do was reply affirmatively to rhetorical questions....

But we were still in the preamble. The first real question came next.

"Can you convince Mark of that?"

Christiane-Sosipatra looked at me again, and this time, I had no doubt who the smile was for. "Does he want to be convinced?" she asked, maliciously.

"He wants to know the truth," Jimmy countered. "He needs to be convinced." He put a slight emphasis on the word *needs*. It wasn't really my supposed need he was talking about. What he meant was that he needed me to be convinced.

Sosipatra stood up then, and came over to the sofa. She only had three strides to travel, but there was something about the way she moved that seemed profoundly unusual, almost uncanny. It wasn't that she was exceptionally graceful—not exactly—but almost as if she wasn't walking at all, but moving purely by the effort of her will, as if she didn't actually need to place her feet on the ground.

I glanced at Jimmy. He was watching me intently, monitoring my reactions—and challenging me, as if to say: "Put a brake on that, Brakeman!"

I didn't move a muscle as Sosipatra leaned over me and stared into my eyes, once I'd shifted my gaze to meet her eyes. The sparkle I'd noticed the first time I had met Christiane was there again, although the quality of the ambient light was quite different.

"Do you want to be convinced, Mark?" she asked, softly—although I had the odd impression that she no more needed to voice the question that she had needed to walk those three paces.

"If it's true," I answered, cautiously. "Then I'll certainly need to be convinced."

I glanced sideways at Claire then. Why? I didn't know. Perhaps I just wanted to break away from the disconcerting mutual stare. Perhaps I wanted to make sure that Claire was there, in case I needed her.

Sosipatra's gaze followed mine momentarily. Christiane was the one who had asked me to being Claire, but that glance told me that whatever reasons Christiane had had in her normal state of consciousness for wanting Claire to be present had become indifferent to her now that she was in Sosipatra mode. I remembered what Christiane had said about Sosipatra's apparent contempt for her, and her consequent feelings of humiliation.

Claire was watching, intently: watching Sosipatra, and watching me. Was there a hint of jealousy in her stare? Perhaps—but there was far more amazement. How often does a twenty-first-century wife get to see a seeress and miracle-worker dead for seventeen hundred years peering into her husband's eyes with that degree of interest?

"How do you feel, Sosipatra?" Jimmy asked.

"Fine," she replied. "You don't have to worry any more, Jim. I know where I am, now. I've got my bearings. I know everything."

"Can you convince Mark of that?" he asked, with just a slight hint of anxiety.

"Yes, my love" she replied. "If he wants to be convinced."

"He does," Jimmy assured her, not bothering, this time, to substitute his need for my desire, effortlessly taking the transition for granted.

"Really?" said Sospitra, looking into my eyes again—but then she moved sideways, in order to stare into Claire's eyes.

"Do *you* want him to be convinced, Claire?" she asked. There was nothing in her tone but curiosity. She wasn't asking for permission to try.

Claire hesitated, and then echoed me: "If it's true, he'll certainly need convincing."

"But you have a risk to run as well, my love," said the seeress. "Even if you weren't here, you'd be at risk. Because he might remember, you see. People can, if they want to, and Mark…I'm not sure that his denial is as solid as he would like to believe. And whether he remembers or not, if I do convince him, even for a moment, it will change him. And that will make a difference to you, Claire, to your life—not to your future, because I can see that and there's no escaping it, but to your thoughts, to your attitude…to your love. It won't make an atom of difference to the pattern of vulgar material causality, but it will make a difference in your soul. Do you want that?"

Claire was a serious person. Even if she thought that it was all non-sense, all game-playing—as I'm certain that she did—she was prepared to play her role. She had asked to be involved, after all.

"No," she replied, "but do it anyway. Do it for him—if that's what he wants." By "him" she meant me. She didn't want Christiane to do it for Jimmy. She wanted her to do it, if she could and if I really wanted it, for me.

The seeress flowed back to me. "Do you want it, Mark?" she asked.

I could simply have said "Yes." I could also have said "No," or even, "I don't know." Which one would have been the honest answer, at that moment in time? I don't know. Probably "I don't know"—but I really don't know, any more than I probably did then.

Instead of answering, I decided to play my own game.

"Explain to me," I said, calmly, "how there can be such things a seeresses, and explain to me how one can seemingly be reincarnated seventeen hundred years after their bodies are dead and buried, in the drugged consciousness of a Médecins Sans Frontières nurse-administrator. If you can even give me a plausible story, then yes, I'm willing to be convinced."

"Willing?" she repeated, staring into my eyes. "Perhaps you don't know yourself as well as you think you do, Mark." She glanced at Claire again, and then at Jimmy; they were both waiting to see her rise to the challenge I'd laid down.

"But if it will help you make up your mind," the seeress in mock-army fatigues continued, "what Mark Two started to tell you ten years ago, in his drug-befuddled, bad-tempered fashion, still confused by far too many other fragments of what you would call his past and future, is true. Human delusions of representing the pinnacle of creation, near to God and made in his image, are ludicrous. Human being is part of a process that extends far into the reaches of the web, a process of recapitulation and refinement, whose templates were formed billions of years ago, in the halo of the star that supplied the raw materials for the star-system that provided the raw materials for the one in which you're located. In one sense, you're a kind of ghost; in another, you're a kind of larva. Your purpose—and there really is a purpose, Mark, an aim, an objective—is to play your tiny part in the production and shaping and perfection of the good, although you're so far away from any inkling of the perfection in question as hardly to be able to begin to imagine it, let alone comprehend it. Your purpose, my love, individually and as a species, is to supply an embryonic phase to the slow development of something superior, physically, mentally and morally. That's all.

"Now, because that's your essential nature, and your essential purpose in the great scheme of things, the genetic make-up of your bodies contains precursors of many of the physical potentials that your descendants' bodies will eventually develop—precursors close enough to be activated by mutation, albeit very rarely, and only partially, because of the inadequacy of their subsequent interaction with the other genes making up your entity. For that reason, humans are occasionally born who have abilities their fellows don't; sometimes, such abilities don't even seem to their fellows to be supernatural, but merely exaggerated—mathematical geniuses are perhaps the most obvious example—but sometimes, too, their talents extend into categories traditionally considered miraculous: psychic communication, transtemopral perception, conscious control of the repair and metamorphosis of the flesh…the list is easy enough to find in the annals of human marvels. Such individuals are greatly misunderstood, of course, even by themselves, but they are real, my love. Sosipatra of Ephesus is real. There are people who can do as much as she did during her incarnation who are alive at what you consider to be this moment in time, although they live in hiding, because that seems to them to be the reasonable thing to do.

"As for my presence here and now—again, speaking in your terms, not mine—you have a very narrow concept of the soul. You've generously expanded it from the old concept that simply equated it with consciousness, to take in the darker fraction of the mind—the unconscious—and when we were talking the other day you were prepared to entertain and toy with the hypothesis that there really might be a sense in which the soul might not merely be immortal in a quasi-linear sense, but ever-present within a closed but tangled loop of eternity. That's getting closer to the reality, I think, but as to imagining, let alone comprehending, the nature of the soul—*the* soul, the universal soul—it's still just scratching the surface."

I glanced at Jimmy. His expression was triumphant. I didn't check on Claire.

"You *think*?" I said to Sosipatra. "You don't *know*?"

"Of course I don't *know*, my love," she said. "I'm only human. For the moment, undoubtedly, with the aid of Jimmy's enhanced entheogen, I'm a slightly cleverer human than you are, but I'm not even truly superhuman, in the sense that all my physical and mental abilities are properly co-ordinated. I'm just a freak, Mark, and a temporary freak at that. I can see a little further into myself and a little further into the web of time than you, but only a little…enough to convince you, though, if that really is what you want…and you needn't tell me that you don't really know, because I know that, because it couldn't be otherwise. But I'd like you at least to try to make up your mind, for your own sake. Do you want me to convince you, yes or no? Are you willing to take the risk? Because if I do, even if you contrive to forget it all afterwards—and you might not—or convince yourself that it was all just a dream and never really happened—and you might not be able to do that either—you'll still be changed. It won't make an atom of difference to the vulgar chain of material causality, but it will change you; it will change your soul."

"Probably?" I queried. "You mean that it *might* change the vulgar chain of material causality? How is that possible, if time is a closed loop, no matter how tangled, in which past, present and future are all one, and eternity is unalterable?"

"Don't be silly, my love. Matter is stubborn, but it's not dead. Of course the loop of eternity is sealed, and the chain of causality unbroken, but that doesn't mean that there's no change, no metamorphosis. *Everything* is in flux, everything is in metamorphosis. There is nothing so absurdly paradoxical as the notion of a static perfection. There's a purpose to all this, Mark—even you can sense that, deep down, no matter how hard you try to deny it, but that doesn't mean that your individual purpose, or desire, or will, has any potency beyond the utterly trivial. If you'll forgive the play on words, my darling, in the cosmic context *you don't matter*. You're of no significance. Nothing you do can make any difference to the pattern, even infinitesimally. Even if the momentary shift in the understanding of your soul can introduce some slight twitch in the chain of causation, it will be just the merest of insignificant twitches. It won't make any difference to the story, to the endeavor, to the purpose."

"Really?" I said. "But sometimes, seemingly insignificant changes can multiply over time, can't they? If a butterfly that flaps its wings in Brazil can occasionally cause a hurricane in the Congo, then what might a tiny change somewhere in the web of eternity cause, if the repercussions extend all the way to perfection?"

I thought that was a good move, if we were playing a game. For an instant, it seemed to give her pause for thought...or pause for something.

Then she said: "You aren't that butterfly, Mark." But she looked into my eyes again, and I had the impression that she could see very clearly that I didn't want to be that butterfly, that I never had and never would. All I wanted was control over my own fragmentary incarnation, my own infinitesimal slice of soul.

She nodded, as if I had said that aloud. But all she said was: "Nor am I."

If I'd been able to read her thoughts the way she seemed to be able to read mine, I was morally certain that I wouldn't have seen see anything like the same complacency, the same lack of desire. I didn't have to glance at Jimmy, either, to know that he *did* want to be that butterfly, even though he wasn't. We were all only human, mere larvae in the process of working our way toward the next phase in a physical and moral metamorphosis that was still a very long way away in the tangled web of time.

"You aren't that butterfly, Mark," Sosipatra repeated, softly. "But if you really do want to be convinced, it will certainly make a difference to *you*, for the twenty-one years seven months and approximately three days that you still have to live. So, once again, ask yourself: *do you want to be convinced?*—because you aren't quite convinced yet, are you, my love?"

I didn't answer that. I didn't have to.

"Approximately?" I queried. "Are you just rounding the numbers off, or are you saying that, for all your miraculous powers, you can't specify the exact moment of my death?"

"Of course I can't specify the exact moment of your death," she said. "Death doesn't have an exact moment. You don't die all at once. The cessation of your heartbeat is only a convenient marker, for record-keeping purposes, and even that's not instantaneous. The cessation of brain activity can take hours, or even days. And the soul goes on, and on...but this is taking too long. Excuse me for a moment."

She drifted away, and went to the wall safe. I watched her, as if mesmerized, unable to take my eyes off her astonishing presence. She opened the safe—one way or another, she obviously knew the combination—and she took out the box of pills. She had no more trouble with the child-proof top that Jimmy had; but she was a professional too, so there was nothing magical about that.

On the other hand….

She looked up at me when she'd opened the box. Then her eyes flickered from side to side, and she smiled, as if she were giving me permission to look away.

I accepted the permission, and followed the directions of her gaze. And suddenly, I felt like a brake-man without a working pedal, in a vehicle that was running away.

Jimmy and Claire were both asleep. Absurd as it might be, in the circumstances—on Jimmy's part, especially—they had nodded off. They weren't snoring, but their eyes were closed and their bodies were relaxed.

I checked the voice-recorder; it was still on; at least, the indicator light was on; it was still recording, obediently.

I wondered, absurdly, whether I ought to tell it what had happened.

It occurred to me that I was now alone, with a botched superhuman who had just taken a second dose of a drug intended to engender a simulacrum of divinity within her.

And just like that, whether I wanted to be or nor, I was convinced that I was out of my existential depth.

XII

"Have you hypnotized them?" I asked, as the seeress took a slight sip of water from the glass to wash down the second pill.

"No," she said. "Why would I? They probably just got bored, because you're getting all the attention. Do you want one yet?" She extended the open pill-box toward me inviting me to hold out my hand to receive one.

"No," I said—and wondered, absurdly, whether I might be asleep too.

"If you really want to be convinced, my love…." There was a mocking edge to her voice, but was still soft and smooth.

"Not that way," I said. "Can you tell me when Jimmy's due to die too, then?"

"Yes, of course. It's nice of you to worry about him. Don't worry, he isn't going to kill himself any time soon. Once again, you win, even though, from your own viewpoint, you lose. He won't outlive you, though. You'll be able to go to his funeral…you and Claire."

She was deliberately teasing me. I hesitated, and then bit the baited hook. "And Melody?" I asked.

"Oh, my love," she said, "there are kinder ways of going about this—kinder to yourself, I mean. But no, your beautiful daughter isn't scheduled for an early death. That doesn't mean, alas, that her life won't have its tragic component. On the other hand, you already know, don't you, that the ecocatastrophe through which she'll have to live her adult life is already unfolding, and can only get worse. You already know that in the course of the next couple of hundred years, the human population of the damaged Earth is going to decline by at least ninety per cent, and that while that's happening, the inhabitants of the developed world are going to have a truly torrid time. But if I were you, dutiful father, I'd try to focus on the good news."

"All right," I said. "Give me the good news."

"The human societies best fitted to survive the crash, as logic will tell you, are the tropical tribesmen who haven't yet lost the arts and practices they'll need to survive when the infrastructure of Western civilization collapses—but that civilization won't be obliterated, Mark. The human world won't revert to the Stone Age, because those primitive cultures, even the misanthropic tribes deep in the Amazon and the hills of Papua New Guinea, have already been polluted and hybridized. They still have the arts and practices they need to survive, but they've also caught a glimpse of civilization, and its ideas and apparatus have already wormed their way to their heads and their way of life. They'll conserve the legacy, nurture it and recapitulate it, with the help of a few survivors who'll be able to hang in the ruins of your society. They two parties will be able to co-operate, to sustain and support one another—and they will. Believe it or not, they will.

"Your particular genetic legacy will be wiped out, obviously, and any intellectual legacy you can leave behind will be infinitesimal, but the human story won't end for a while yet, and the human component of the universal soul still has a role to play, a contribution to make to the purpose. I hope you can be glad about that, my love, because, having accepted this challenge, I really would like you to be glad about something, and to be perfectly honest, if you really do want to be convinced, it isn't going to make a contribution to the sum of your happiness. But you know that, and you're doing it anyway.

"Now, that really is enough chitchat. All of that is too easily forgettable, too easily dismissed as the stuff of dreams. If you do want to be convinced, we need to go beyond that. If you really are ready to be convinced...."

She stopped talking. Then she took her clothes off, stripping completely naked.

She didn't say anything, but she gave the impression of being relieved to be free of the encumbrance, even though the shell-suit she'd been wearing had been as comfortable as clothing gets nowadays. She passed her hands lightly over her body, and breathed deeply.

Then she went into the kitchen, and came back with a sharp knife.

I was paralyzed—perhaps not literally, but what difference does it make? I couldn't move.

This time, I knew, there wasn't going to be a wrestling match. This time, I was a brake-man without a working brake-pedal. I knew that if she plunged that blade into her forehead or her eye, I wasn't going to be able to stop her, to matter how sorry I felt for poor Christiane. I literally wasn't going to be able to stop her.

She looked down at her left forearm, but shook her head briefly, as if remembering that Jimmy hadn't been able to impress me with that in the Roebuck ten years before.

Then she looked at me. "Don't worry, my love," she said. "I know that you're not quite convinced yet, viscerally speaking, but you know, deep down, that I'm really not going to hurt myself with *this*. She held up the blade for the sake of emphasis—and then she stabbed herself in the abdomen, twisted the knife, drew it in a horizontal arc, and allowed her intestines to flow out through the horrible gash she'd made, although she caught the slithering section in her left hand before it could dangle all the way to the floor. Then she showed me the red blade, dripping blood, before she set it down on the table.

She was at least four yards away, but she didn't walk the intervening distance. She floated.

"Well then, St. Thomas," she said, as she brought me to my feet, and picked up my hand. "Stick it in."

I didn't—but she did. She pushed my hand into the gaping, bleeding wound, through and among the tangled web of her guts, which were still trying to follow the dictates of the law of gravity and spill out in a serpentine cataract.

"Visceral enough for you, my darling?" she asked, sardonically.

My hand was actually inside her body, in amongst the living offal and the wet, reeking blood.

Was I convinced? Absolutely.

Deep down, though, I suppose that some fragment of my soul must have realized that the very unthinkability of it would make it easier for me, at some later point in what still seemed to me to be the relentless flow of time, to think that it *must* have been a dream and a delusion, because it *couldn't* really have happened…especially when she took my hand out again, released it, pushed back the leaking intestines, and passed her hand over the cut again, sealing it.

She picked up the knife and licked the blade clean of blood. Then she got down on all fours and licked up the blood that had spilled on to the table-top. There was still some soaking into the carpet, but she passed her hand over the stains, and they vanished.

I looked at my hand. It was red and it was sticky—but only for a moment. Whether it was my hand that absorbed the blood or whether the blood made its own way into my veins I couldn't tell. Did it make any difference?

I looked at Sosipatra again.

"It's only blood," she said. "Vulgar matter. That's not what will make a difference to you."

I looked back at the clean hand. That, I thought, *had* to be an illusion. It had to be a trick. Later, some part of me already knew, I would be able to tell myself that I had been "hypnotized," or employ some other explanatory fudge, some figurative Polyfilla, in order to block or paper over the crack in my understanding. *It couldn't be real.*

But at the time, I was convinced that it was perfectly real. As with St. Thomas, if he had ever existed at all, let alone whether he had been a former incarnation of my own rubber soul, my doubt had melted away.

I tore my gaze away from my hand again, in order to confront what I was still stubbornly endeavoring to think of as Christiane's face—but it was no longer Christiane's face, or Sosipatra's.

It was Melody's.

Seeing her stab herself in the abdomen and then unstab herself hadn't made my blood run cold, and it hadn't sent an electric frisson running through me, because I'd known what was coming, vaguely—but seeing Melody standing there, stark naked, even when I knew that it wasn't really her, but merely Sosipatra metamorphosed or glamorized, was like being kicked in the chest by a horse. My heart stopped momentarily. I couldn't breathe.

I hadn't seen Melody naked since she was seven years old. We weren't the kind of family whose members walked in casually on one another in the bathroom; we respected one another's modesty. I had never seen my daughter naked as a young woman, and certainly not as an immodest young woman who was literally displaying herself for my inspection.

I shut my eyes.

"All right," I said. "That's enough."

I sat down again, on the sofa, beside Claire, who didn't stir.

Later, I knew, I'd be able to tell myself that it had been a delusion. But at the time, when my tormentor reached out and stroked my face gently with her hand, the hand I felt was my beloved daughter's hand, and the voice I heard saying, yet again: "Do you want to be convinced, Mark?" was my beloved daughter's voice.

And I said: "Yes," knowing full well what it was that I was agreeing to.

She moved away, and when I opened my eyes again, it was Christiane/Sosipatra who was standing in front of me, with a glass that still contained half an inch of water in her right hand, and a little white pill in the open palm of her left.

It could have been anything. It could have even been a placebo. I told myself that as I put it on my tongue, took a sip of water and swallowed it. But I didn't believe it.

Nothing happened immediately, of course. Everything takes time. Even dying, I'd just been assured, takes a lot longer than we imagine, even though we're not consciously aware of its temporal extension, and I believed it. The brain takes time to adjust to being dead, and it lets go of the physicality of existence slowly. And the soul goes on. Except that "going on" is just an illusion of the sensorium, because in the realm of the hyperreal, the vast soul just *is*, and always has been, and always will be, within the mysterious process of its eternal metamorphosis, its enigmatic quest for the holy grail of the good.

"It's bound to be confusing, the first time, my love," said Sosipatra, now kneeling down in front of the sofa and leaning forward to place her folded arms in my lap, and looking up at me, "but I'll try to help you make sense of it, as best I can, because I'd like you to be able to understand as much as you can, in order to be convinced, at least for the moment. Perhaps you'll forget it all later, and perhaps you'll convince yourself that it was just a drug-induced bout of insanity, but I know that, subconsciously if not consciously, you really would like to be convinced, and that you really might cling on to the memory, as best you can. Can you smell something?"

For a moment, I thought she was asking whether I could sense the odor of her own body, exposed to the air, or the reek of blood that had snatched at my nostrils while her guts were spilling out—but then I sensed the odor that she was expecting me to apprehend. It was like nothing I had ever smelled before. I knew that it wasn't really an odor at all, in the sense of airborne chemical particles intercepted by the mucus of the nasal membranes. It was in my head, rising from the unconscious; my consciousness was simply construing what was happening physically in my brain as the perception of an odor.

And so it began. The doors of perception opened, not smoothly, but relentlessly.

The odor wasn't unpleasant, but nor was it sweet.

"That's the perfume of time," she told me. "We usually call trans-temporal perception *seeing*, and those who are able to do it *seers*, but your brain is far more versatile than that. The conscious component of all five senses becomes engaged when a refined entheogen takes effect— odor first and then…can you feel the rest beginning to kick in? Can you taste eternity?"

I could. Eternity isn't sweet either—strangely salty, in fact, reminiscent of oceanic brine.

"Can you see what you used to call the future and the past?"

I could but it was kaleidoscopically confused, full of color and light, with only fugitive flashes of recognition, which might have been an effect of desperation.

"It becomes clearer, by degrees," she assured me. "Imagine what it must be like for a blind man suddenly gifted with sight. You have to learn to make sense of it all, to build the connections with what you know. Can you hear the music of time, the harmony of the galaxies?"

I could certainly hear something, and I was prepared to suppose that it might be music of a sort, but it didn't seem very melodic. Again, it wasn't sweet, or soothing.

"Most of all, my love can you feel the touch of time? Can you feel the thrill of time, the eroticism of time?"

I could. I understood, then, why she had taken her clothes off. She hadn't touched herself in any of her everyday erogenous zones, and when she had stabbed herself with the knife, she hadn't been mimicking the sexual act in some perverse fashion. She hadn't had to do anything like that, and it would have been absurd if she had, because the eroticism of time wasn't that kind of crude local friction, that kind of primitive symbolic representation. It wasn't confined to particular organs, to arousal and orgasm; it was far more fundamental than that. The touch of time eroticized all flesh, and more. The thrill of time was....

Yes, this time, it *was* sweet, and soothing.

She moved aside in order to allow me to get up, and to take off my own clothes.

We didn't *do* anything. We didn't even look at one another. It wasn't an orgy. But I was glad, even so, that Claire's eyes were closed. I wasn't being unfaithful to her, certainly not with Sosipatra, nor with Christiane, nor with the universe. But Claire might well have thought that I wasn't observing our usual standards of decency.

For a moment or two, I thought that Claire might have been right to ask Jimmy whether she could try out his magic potion. For a moment, I thought that she might like it, might even benefit from it...but only for a moment.

As Sosipatra had said, it all took what I have previously considered to be time. The pseudosensory impressions didn't all come at once. The perfume, the music, and the total erotic bliss came one by one, overlapping but not simultaneous...and the spectrum didn't end there.

There was also the terror, or, more accurately, the horror.

I remembered, belatedly, than the mental entity that Jimmy had dredged up with the aid of the ayahuasca derivative had been, at least for a substantial interval, in an utterly foul mood, and when I sensed the cosmic horror flooding my altered consciousness, I realized why.

I realized, too, why Mark Two had hinted that Jimmy might be a fool for thinking that it if he did manage to open the doors of perception wide, he would like what he found beyond them, or even be able to tolerate it.

I gasped, and wanted to die simply to get away from it.

Infinity is intimidating and overwhelming. It crushes you. As for eternity...*here be dragons* doesn't even begin to describe it, nor Jimmy's glib Nietzschean quote about what happens when you look into the abyss. Presumably, Nietzsche thought he knew whereof he spoke—but he didn't have a refined entheogen with which to fathom it.

I realized, briefly, what a truly bad idea existence is, and why it would be so much better if nothing existed rather than something. I wondered how Sosipatra, and those like her, could stand it.

I was an idiot, but for the moment, I was in no condition even to see the obvious. There is, however, a spectrum, and everything was still in metamorphosis, as it always is.

"Hold on, my love," said Sosipatra, reaching out to place her warm hands over my clenched fists. "It's just part of it. You'll accommodate it, just as you accommodate everything else. It sometimes helps to talk, I find, even though you can get seriously irritated if people ask you stupid questions; it's better to remain in control, to the extent that you can. You're beginning to understand, aren't you, why people who have access to it, however partial or fragmentary, are wise to dissimulate? You're beginning to understand why there's a truly profound wisdom in the normal, everyday consciousness that wants to shut it out completely…but you can also understand, can't you, how strong the temptation becomes, how strong the addiction becomes, if you have an addictive personality. You don't have that, I think…but poor Christiane does."

I used my forefingers to wipe away tears from my cheeks.

"My God!" I said, with feeling.

"That is one way of putting it," she agreed. "Maybe not the best way, but it helps. All the words help, in fact, no matter how nonsensical they might seem when you sober up. It's hit you hard, I can tell…but not too hard. You're strong, Mark—stronger than Jim, I suspect. And you're not alone in life, as he is, even when he's got someone like me. You have existential anchorages, and you know how precious they are. You have to take the rough with the smooth, and because of the way the universe is, at least in this phase of its tangled eternity, there's more rough than smooth, but we're intelligent beings; we have iron in the soul.

"Concentrate on the smooth, and you'll probably be fine…as fine as it gets. You can't screen out the horror, obviously, but you can learn to focus on the erotic, and the sight, once you learn to use it. Concentrate on the sight, Mark, or the hearing, for the moment, if that's easier. Ultimately, it's just a matter of taste. I don't have much of an ear for music myself, but I suspect that some people can really lose themselves in the music of time, and that's what they combine with the eroticism in order to find their personal shadow of fulfillment. I really am a seeress, though; always have been always will be, over and over and over again. I can see more clearly than is good for me, but you can't take your mind's eyes away once you've got a grip. Once you can see, you can't unsee…so concentrate on the music, at least for now. Is this helping? I'll shut up if you prefer."

"No," I said, feebly. "It would be too confusing. Please keep talking. Maybe I don't have an ear for the music of eternity either. I need a voice; I need guidance. I need answers…."

"You already have the answers, Mark. You always have had the answers. It's just a matter of teasing them out, if you really want to know what they are. What most people need, I think, like poor Mark Two, is the questions, because without those to spur them on and focus their attention, they can't get their bearings. I don't have that problem…Sosipatra doesn't have it, I mean. She's already laid the foundations, you see, deep in the recesses of Christiane's fragment of the soul. Delivering her was a great deal easier than it was for Jim to engender Mark Two. Do you have a sense of alternative identity yet, Mark? It's not really necessary, but I suspect that it sometimes helps."

"No," I said. "I'm not remembering any past lives…except…I remember *myself*, I remember myself, extending back it into antiquity… but I don't seem to have a particular period…just a kind of overview, as if the individualized fragments mattered so little, having been so insignificant, that I've discarded the specifics of their existence and just retained their sense of their position in the pattern. Comes of being a historian, I guess…or, at least, the kind of historian I've always been… and maybe always will be…"

"Maybe, Mark?"

"Definitely maybe," I told her. "I'm not willing to admit, yet, that my powers of personal metamorphosis are a feeble as you imply."

"Good," she said. "Hang on to that conviction, Mark, if you can. Maybe it's foolish, but what do I know? I'm only human…and in the fullness of time…just a momentary entity, utterly ephemeral."

I wasn't really paying attention when she moved away; I was too overwhelmed, lost in the perception of eternity…or at least the infinitesimally tiny fragment of it to which my enhanced senses gave me access. I was only peripherally aware of the fact that she'd picked up the pill-box again, opened the drinks cabinet, taken out the bottle of whisky and filled the glass that had previously contained water with liquor.

I don't know how many pills she took—more than one, obviously. A lot. Too many.

With the aid of hindsight, I can understand now that she probably wasn't really paying attention either—not to herself, certainly not to her Christiane self-fragment, and probably not to her Sosipatra-fragment either. She was engrossed in her project, engrossed in convincing me of the reality of what she was, and what we all are.

Why?

Good question. I think, somehow, she—meaning both Sosipatra and Christiane—needed that for her own psychological purposes. Like Mark Two, she needed some kind of stimulus to help her orientate herself within herself, for the magnified moment that that Jimmy's drug had provoked and magnified. She wasn't convincing me in order to please Jimmy, let alone for my benefit. It was more self-centered than that, perhaps more perverse.

There was a reason, though, for that and...the rest. There was a purpose. And somehow, no matter how irrational, or perverse, or evil it seemed, from some viewpoints, ultimately, it was all in the service of the good, in the great cause of the perfection of perfection.

God alone knows how; I certainly don't—but you have to cling on to the available straws, and hope that they can save you from drowning.

"Do you want another?" she asked me, offering a pill in her open palm.

"No," I said. "I don't think I could take any more."

"You do," she prophesied, "in time." But she dropped the pill she was holding back into the box and put the box back on the table. Then she drained the glass. There had been a lot of whisky in it, but she downed the lot in one gulp.

"You've stopped weeping," she observed. "I told you that you'd accommodate it, didn't I?"

"Yes," I agreed.

"It's like everything else. You get used to it—and then you get to like it, to need it, to be unable to do without it. You're lucky, I suspect, because you've had love in your life for a long time. Your wife loves you, and your daughter loves you. Christiane really envies you that, and not because she'd like to bed your daughter, or your wife, or you, but...well, I think you understand what I mean, by now. She's never had anything stable in her life, anything she could rely on. Sex, yes, love...maybe just a little, but nothing remotely comparable to what the eroticism of eternity provides. That's something of which she was always starved even of the faintest echo. She likes Jim, obviously, but you know what scares her about that, don't you?"

"Yes," I said.

"I know you do. The mists are beginning to clear, aren't they? You're beginning to work your way through the confusion? You've got past the horror, haven't you?"

I hadn't. You never get past the horror. She knew that—but she also knew that I no longer wanted to die just to get away from it. She understood.

"Well," she added, "you're beginning to learn to live with it, anyway. And as I was saying, you know what I mean about Christiane and Jim. You know that he was far more to Christiane than just body parts to stick into herself for the sake of a petty thrill."

I hadn't quite caught on to the entire logic of the fact that she was talking about herself in the third person. She was being Sosipatra the seeress, obviously, but that wasn't the whole of it, and in not yet seeing the rest, I was being stupid. No matter how far we learn to see into hyperreality, our blindness always remains infinite, and sometimes much closer to home than we'd care to admit. But I did know what she meant about Jimmy, and why Christiane was scared.

"He's your supplier," I said. "He's your connection."

"That's right. And what would have happened, do you think, when he decided that his little experiment had come to an end. What would have happened when he's achieved his primary objective, when he'd succeeded? What would have happened, do you think, when Christiane had served her purpose, and convinced you that Jim was right all along, and won him his stupid, perverted private game?"

Her use of the future conditional tense was a joke, because she knew that in the limited sense that there really is a future, it isn't conditional—not for the likes of us. We aren't that butterfly. She knew, too, that I knew what she meant. I had worked it out, with the aid of her prompting.

"But he loves you," I objected, I knew that it wasn't an adequate objection, but it was reflexive. And who, in any case, was *you*?

She didn't even bother to deny it, or dismiss it as irrelevant.

You have to remember that she wasn't quite herself. She was Sosipatra of Ephesus, in part. But she was Christiane too. She had Christiane's fears, and Christiane's disappointment with her life, Christiane's sense of being, Christiane's loneliness. She might feel contempt for Christiane, but it didn't alter that fact that she was who she was.

While she was speaking, she had slowly got dressed again. That was considerate of her, but she could see the unconditional future. She knew how the situation was going to play out, in unreal time. She didn't want Claire, or the paramedics, or anyone else, to know that she'd been naked. She wanted to smooth things over for us, to the extent that they could be smoothed over. She was being considerate.

There was no point in protesting. It was already done. It had always been done, and had always been inevitable. There was absolutely nothing that I, or Jimmy, or Christiane or Sosipatra of Ephesus could have done to induce even the slightest swerve in the great chain of causation that extents for trillions of trillions of trillions of years through our tiny loop of the tangled web of time. How could we? How could anyone, even the cosmic engineer?

But still, I felt that had to ask, not for clarification but for endorsement.

"Why?"

She sighed. "Why indeed? But there is a purpose, Mark. Somewhere, and somewhen, there's a purpose, and it's all for the cause of the good, for the sake of the perfection of perfection."

And then she dropped dead.

Except, of course, that she couldn't. You can't just drop dead; it takes time. You can't just die. In fact, you can't really die at all. You don't have that option, even if you disembowel yourself with a carving knife and don't bother to stick yourself back together again and suck up all the blood, so as not to leave an inconvenient mess. Even that wouldn't be terminal, but merely a transient punctuation mark in the sentence of the soul. Nor is simply instructing your heart to stop, or feeding it an overdose of whisky-soaked entheogen.

The flesh is weak; the flesh melts away, just as time itself sometimes appears to do, but even fragile, temporary consciousness can recur, and almost certainly will, somewhen along the tangle—although whether any of us can or should feel the slightest crumb of comfort in that conviction is another matter entirely.

XIII

I got dressed. I pocketed the box of pills. I thought about erasing the voice-recording, but I didn't. I figured that I might as well let Jimmy have it, and allow him to make of it what he would.

Then I snapped my fingers. It was just a symbolic gesture; it wasn't the sound of the snap that brought Claire and Jimmy out of their trance; if it really was my act of will that unhypnotized them, it didn't need any physical support.

They both reacted as people do who have dropped off momentarily and whose first reaction, on recovering consciousness, is to deny that they'd ever lost it. They looked startled. Then they looked round. Then they saw Christiane lying on the floor, dead, or at least in the terminal phase of dying, her consciousness dissolved.

They both leapt to their feet. "What happened?" Claire demanded, anxiously but not hysterically. She went into first aid mode, but she knew that it was hopeless as soon as she touched the dead flesh that had been Christiane.

I was still under the influence of Jimmy's magic potion. I knew exactly how the scene had to play out, in unreality.

"Call 999, Jim," I said. "Ask for an ambulance, tell the operator that Christiane's collapsed, and that you can't be sure whether she's still breathing. They'll keep you on the line. When they've scrambled the paramedic ambulance, they'll ask you lots of stupid questions and give you some pointless instructions, which Claire is already following. Do everything they tell you. Don't worry. The autopsy and the toxicology report won't reveal anything. The medical examiner will jump to some convenient fudge along the line of sudden heart failure due to undiagnosed congenital weakness. Switch off your voice-recorder, but leave it where it is. Nobody is going to ask whether it was on or ask you to play it back. Just tell them the fundamental, elementary truth: that we came back here after lunch, that we sat down, that we were talking, that Christiane had a glass of whisky, but that you didn't notice anything out of the ordinary until she collapsed. There'll be a ton of hassle, obviously, but it will all blow over."

Jimmy was looking at me as if he didn't recognize me, but he did as he was told. He was tied up on the phone for the next twenty-five minutes, going through the rigmarole while the ambulance made its way from Basingstoke, because Fleet Ancillary Station was temporarily off-line.

In the meantime, Claire buttonholed me, and said: "But what happened, Mark? I didn't even see her fall down. She was just talking—just trying to convince you that you ought to want to be convinced. I didn't see her drink any whisky."

"She did," I assured her. "But you're right. She was just talking, trying to convince me that I ought to want to be convinced. And then she collapsed. She always knew, though, that she was playing with fire, and that Jimmy's assurances about his compound being safe weren't reliable. She always knew that it might happen."

That was understating the case, but I was trying to operate on a need to know basis. After all, Christiane had been right. I loved Claire and she loved me, and that was invaluable. She was my anchorage, and I knew how precious it was to have an anchorage of that kind, especially if you undertake odysseys in hyperreality, deliberately or accidentally.

We followed the ambulance to the hospital in Jimmy's car. Technically, he was probably over the limit, but he'd sobered up completely—and I mean completely. He'd reached a phase in his obsession where it would have taken more than seventeen stitches in his best friend's face to put him off, but this was an order of magnitude worse. In his view, he's just killed his collaborator and lover.

He had, in a sense. There was a sense, too, in which she had killed herself. But there was also another sense in which neither of them was in the least responsible,. It had always been built into the relentless chain of causality, which has no beginning and no end, and is so heavy that it's almost impossible to twitch.

It was just one of those things—but even within the context of our pathetically tiny nexus, it wasn't devoid of purpose, or entirely devoid of the good. Jimmy had sobered up, entirely. He wasn't going to kill himself any time soon. And I....

I had caught a glimpse of hyperreality. Perhaps the change that it had wrought in me wouldn't work entirely to my benefit, but, as Christiane had said, while she was still herself, it was something I'd rather have than not have. Darkness is more comfortable than enlightenment, for sleeping, but the temptation of the latter is simply too powerful, even when it's dangerous, or deadly.

We were all present when Christiane was pronounced dead on arrival at the hospital. She'd been dead for some time by then, of course, technically speaking, but these things have to be pronounced by the book.

Jimmy stayed with her in the morgue while Claire and I took a taxi home. Claire asked me questions all the way, none of which I wanted to answer, but she didn't seem disappointed, because she accepted at face value my assertion that I couldn't. She still trusted me, and I still loved her. Like Jimmy, we would endure, for the tiny span of apparent time that remained to us, providing one another with invaluable mutual support. Eventually, the questions would dwindle away, as she realized that perhaps it was better not to know the answers.

Melody was surprised to see us back so soon, but we didn't catch her doing anything that she wasn't suppose to be doing. It was still early, mind.

When we told her that Christiane had collapsed suddenly and died, she wept.

"It was the drug, wasn't it?" she asked.

"Yes, it was," I said, "but it won't show up in any toxicology analysis. Jimmy won't be in any trouble, if we all keep quiet about it. It won't be difficult. There won't be a police investigation, just an inquest. I'll have to give evidence, but it will all be a matter of going through the motions. There are no suspicious circumstances. It was just one of those things."

I still had the pill-box in my pocket. When Jimmy played the tape back, whether he did that before or after checking the safe, he'd know that Christine had taken more pills, and that I'd taken one before refusing a second. He might jump to the conclusion that I must have taken the remaining pills, but he had no proof.

He'd ask me about it, obviously, just as he'd ask me what I'd experienced, given that almost all the words recorded on the tape were Christiane's, but I already knew that I'd be able to put him off, not just in the metaphorical sense, but in the sense that the temptation to cook up more of the drug and take it himself wouldn't be strong enough actually to make him do it. I would be able to persuade him that although the drug was a powerful hallucinogen, which did indeed communicate the impression of being able to see through time, albeit in a directly confused and incomprehensible fashion, the supposed enlightenment thus gained wasn't worth the price of admission.

I was able to do all that quite skillfully, in a sly and subtle fashion, partly because I was able to convince him that he had won the game he'd been playing for thirty years, that he'd won me over…as, in a sense, he had.

And, as Christiane or Sosipatra had prophesied, I didn't forget.

I could have, but I didn't. Perhaps I still could, if I put my mind to it, but I won't. Some dreams—including some nightmares—really do need to be remembered, even if that's all they are. The question is, do I want to be convinced that that is all it was? *Can* I convince myself of that, even if I want to?

Left to himself, Jimmy would probably not have played the tape to Claire, but he wasn't left to himself, of course. She made him play it to her. I didn't object. She listened to it all, and doubtless made some correct deductions, and must have inferred, too, that there was an awful lot going on that wasn't described verbally, but I didn't volunteer any information and, on due reflection, she must have decided that it was best to bring the *don't ask don't tell* rule back into play, at least for a while.

She looks at me differently now, because she knows that I'm different, albeit subtly, but it hasn't made any different to her fundamental feelings, or to the routines of her behavior. The vulgar pattern of cause and effect goes stubbornly on…although that might not always be the case. One day, she might insist on knowing, and I won't have the right to deny her a full explanation.

And that's one of the reasons why I've taken the trouble to write it all down, now that Jimmy has finished his leave, and won't be dropping round the house every couple of days or so to ask me maudlin questions about my last poignant hour with his lover, the texture of time, the nature of universe and the purpose of it all, and to cast occasional lustful, or at least wistful, glances at Claire and Melody, whenever they happen to be around.

He's been posted back to Indonesia, but to Sumatra rather than Papua New Guinea. Perhaps the company psychologists thought that Jiwaka might have too many painful memories for him, and reduce his commitment to his work, and hence his productivity. Perhaps they're right.

There are, I suppose, other reasons for making a full record. I won't show it to Claire unless she asks, but I do have an idea in the back of my mind that perhaps I ought to leave it to Melody, as a kind of perverse legacy, to read after I'm gone. Then again, Christiane was all alone in the world, except for Jimmy, Sosipatra and us. Nobody really cared about her passing, or even noticed it, except for the five of us and a handful of people in Jiwaka. The vast majority of human lives, of course, go unrecorded, and even those that are recorded are very rarely comprehended to any real degree, and perhaps I ought to be glad to have the opportunity to set her record straight, as a kind of memorial.

But when all is said and done, the primary purpose of setting it all down is to help me to make my own judgment, as to what I ought to think about it all, and what it might be possible to think about it all.

There's a sense, you see, in which the central, fundamental question still needs to be answered. Do I really want to be convinced? And if so, of what? The options of conviction still remain open, and perhaps always will. Was it all just bullshit, just a crazy hallucination dredged up from the stinking, horrific, perversely eroticized depths of my stagnant subconscious, or was it, and is it, quite real? Was it, and is it, true?

There's no way of knowing, obviously. I still have the pills, and I could take another, or all of them, carefully spaced out in order to limit their toxicity. But I don't have to, in spite of what Sosipatra prophesied. And what could it prove, in the final analysis, except the ingenuity of my imagination?

But the prophetess was right about the fundamental issue. Whether I decide to be convinced or not, the experience has changed me. Even though it hasn't made an atom of difference to the chain of causality—I still get up very morning, shower, have breakfast, go to school, come home, have dinner, sleep with my wife, and look forward with trepidation to the imminent day when my beloved daughter will be leaving home to go to university, all the way to London, more than thirty miles away—the person doing all those things isn't the same person who used to do them. Anyone you ask will still tell you that he's the sanest person they know, and perhaps they're right, by any definition that can be sensibly applied, but he's not the same sane person as before. Once the divine within has been engendered, it can't be unengendered. I'm changed, forever…and ever.

Am I glad about that? Not particularly, but I'm not sorry either. It was, after all, inevitable.

When I think about Christiane, as I do sometimes, I feel sad, but not surprised. It seems to me, on reflection, that she had volunteered for Jimmy's ludicrous project precisely because she knew that it would end the way it did. I'm sure in my own mind that she knew that what she did would enable Jimmy to set his lifelong obsession aside, or at least become sufficiently careful in its pursuit that he didn't destroy himself, but I'm not at all sure she was trying to save him from himself, any more than she was trying to save me. She was an angel of sorts in Jiwaka, but not in Church Crookham.

It also seems to me, on further reflection, that Jimmy had never really wanted me to sit with him in order that he might be protected from harm, or even to prove something to me, but merely to serve as a witness to his bizarre adventures in extremism, to react to his performances, without him caring overmuch what the reaction was, as long as he got one, after the fashion of an attention-seeking child. When his sideshow—because it really was a sideshow, in spite of what he said—got Christiane killed, the thrill went out of the game, and he won't need it any more in future. I suspect, though, that whether I see ever see him again or not, I'll be ever-present in his imagination: always watching him over his shoulder, always braking his flights of fancy when they go too fast or too far.

I suspect, too—in fact I'm certain—that I'll be able to put Jimmy out of my mind far more firmly than he'll been able to put me out of his, if that's what I want. Even though I'm the one who still bears the scar of our early friendship, I'm well able to live my life unobserved by any troublesome imaginary inquisitor. I've been able to build an authentically adult self, and to position that authentic self securely and productively within the "real" world, solidly anchored by love. My life has always been a success, and my success has been so obvious, so comfortable and so complete that I'd never needed the endorsement of anyone who'd known me when I was nothing but a mere bundle of hopes and ambitions. Jimmy hasn't had that. Jimmy has been frustrated all his life, like Christiane, or like a metaphorical Oliver Twist unable to find his real family or his true destiny.

All I have to do, now, is just keep on going. I don't have to change anything more. Everything is in place. And if I need anything to remind me of the wisdom of the life I've made, and the good of the life I have, I only have to think about Jimmy, and Christiane, and what an unholy mess they made of things, in order to help me feel smug.

In life, I still tell myself every day, you have to resist the allure of extremes. That way lies madness. You have to learn to be content with what you can have, and shut your eyes to all the illusions and all the great unknowns. You have to learn to trust yourself, and be glad you're what you are, even if you know that you're just an infinitesimal larva in a process of metamorphosis that can only reach perfection at some unimaginably distant location in the tangled web of time. That's the only kind of happy ending there can be, or ever will be, believe me.

I'm not the hypothetical allegorical butterfly of chaos theory. None of us is. We're only human, only larvae.

But I still have that pill-box, and it still contains nine pills, and I know that if I ever do take another, I'll be able to adapt more rapidly and more securely to the altered state of conscious they confer. I'll be able to make more progress, whether I have anyone to ask me questions or not.

My old self would have thrown them away by now, of course, or carefully denatured them with fire or strong acid, but I'm not the person I used to be, and I never will be again.

So that's the end—insofar as there can be an end, to this or any other story.

www.ingramcontent.com/pod-product-compliance
Lightning Source LLC
Chambersburg PA
CBHW050759250626
47155CB00005B/2129